Mystery of the Lost Heirloom

BOOKS BY RUTH NULTON MOORE

The Sara and Sam Series
  Mystery of the Missing Stallions
  Mystery of the Secret Code
  Mystery of the Lost Heirloom

Other Junior High Books
  Danger in the Pines
  The Ghost Bird Mystery
  In Search of Liberty
  Mystery at Indian Rocks
  Mystery of the Lost Treasure
  Peace Treaty
  The Sorrel Horse
  Wilderness Journey

For Younger Readers
  Tomás and the Talking Birds
  Tomás y los Pajaros Párlantes (Spanish)

Mystery of the Lost Heirloom

Ruth Nulton Moore

Illustrated by James Converse

Sara and Sam Series, Book 3

HERALD PRESS
Scottdale, Pennsylvania
Kitchener, Ontario
1986

Library of Congress Cataloging-in-Publication Data

Moore, Ruth Nulton.
    Mystery of the lost heirloom.

    (Sara and Sam series ; bk. 3)
    Summary: While accompanying their father to
Wyalusing, Pennsylvania, to do research on a French
refugee settlement of 200 years ago, twins Sam and
Sara become involved in a search for the valuable
stolen pendant of an Indian princess.
    [1. Mystery and detective stories.   2. Twins—
Fiction.   3. Pennsylvania—Fiction.   4. Indians of
North America—Fiction]   I. Converse, James, ill.
II. Title.   III. Series: Moore, Ruth Nulton, Sara and
Sam series ; bk. 3.
PZ7.M7878Mxk   1986   [FIC]   85-27334

MYSTERY OF THE LOST HEIRLOOM
Copyright © 1986 by Herald Press, Scottdale, Pa. 15683
    Published simultaneously in Canada by Herald Press,
    Kitchener, Ont. N2G 4M5. All rights reserved.
Library of Congress Catalog Card Number: 85-27334
International Standard Book Number: 0-8361-3408-7
Printed in the United States of America
Design by Alice B. Shetler

91 90 89 88 87 86 10 9 8 7 6 5 4 3 2 1

To my son,
Carl Nulton Moore,
who likes history, too

Contents

Author's Note

THE Grand Spiritual and Temporal Council of the North American Indians, the first in 208 years, was held at the Wyalusing Prayer Rocks in 1963. I visited the council at that time and have used it as a model for the Grand Council meeting in this book. Chief Sun Bear and Princess Morning Star in my story are fictitious, although there were three chiefs and a lovely Indian princess at the Grand Spiritual Council of 1963.

Anyone in Wyalusing, searching for Charles and Blair LaRue and their Victorian house, will not find them, for they, too, are imaginary. However, the town of Wyalusing, Pennsylvania, the Wyalusing Prayer Rocks, Spirit Lake, and the council grounds, now a private residence, can be found in the beautiful Endless Mountains of Pennsylvania. Also the Marie Antoinette Lookout, Homet's Ferry, and French Azilum, along the Susquehanna River, are very real and fascinating places to visit.

I wish to thank Martha Hermann Hagermann, curator of French Azilum, for her help in locating Homet's Ferry; Jean and Jim Caine for letting me use their inn, guest cottages,

and gift shop at the Marie Antoinette Lookout for back-
ground material for my story; and Nicholas Herzog, his
pony, Ginger, and goat, Pearl, for showing me around the
council grounds as it is today.

Mystery of the
Lost Heirloom

1
A Mystery to Solve

HOW would you all like to go to Wyalusing?" Professor Harmon asked his family.

It was a warm June evening, and the Harmons were eating dinner in their old stone farmhouse at Marsh Pond Farm.

Sara and Sam stared with surprise at their father, and so did their older brother, Tim. Yet they were not all that surprised. It seemed that when Dad had anything important to announce, he always liked to announce it suddenly, like dropping a thought bomb, right in the middle of dinner.

"Wya—what?" Sara asked. Such an unusual name. She had never heard it before.

"Wyalusing," Dad said, grinning. "It's an old Indian

name for a small town in the Endless Mountains. The native Americans called the original town, M'chwihillusing, which meant 'the place of the old man.' "

"Another history lesson," Tim groaned as he reached for a roll.

Sara was all smiles. "Yeah, Dad, school's out for the summer."

Sam cocked his head, puzzled. "Why should we like to go to Wyalusing, Dad?"

Professor Harmon drew a letter from his pocket and opened it. "I'm researching material for an article on old French Azilum, which is across the river from Wyalusing," he told them, handing the letter to Mom. "I remembered that a college friend of mine, Charles LaRue, owns a lumber company in Wyalusing, so I wrote to him for information. He wrote back that they are restoring the old French colony and that I should come to Wyalusing to see it for myself. He invited us all to stay with him and his son for a week."

Mom read the letter quickly, then handed it back to Dad. "But, John, bringing the whole family would be an imposition."

"I thought so, too, so I telephoned Charles this morning and told him that just I would be coming. But he insisted that you all should come. He said his house is large enough to accommodate us and that he'd like our families to meet. Charles is like that. He's one of the most friendly persons I know."

Mom drew in a long breath. "Well, I don't know, John...."

"Oh, I know it'll be all right," Dad assured her. "Charles told me that he's a widower now, and he and his only child, Blair, live with a housekeeper in the big ancestral home. He said he and Blair like to have young people around."

"I guess by young people that means us," Sam spoke up.

"That's right," Professor Harmon answered his younger son with a half chuckle, "although your mother and I aren't exactly ancient."

"Well, I can't go," Tim reminded them all. "I got a job this summer at the Rabers."

"And you wouldn't want to leave Vickie for a whole long week," Sam teased, referring to the Rabers' pretty daughter who was the same age as Tim.

All this time Sara sat quietly thinking of the gentle gray mare at the Rabers' stable. "I have a job, sort of, too," she spoke up. "Who's going to exercise Dusty while we're away?"

"How about your friend, Amy?" Dad asked. "I'm sure she wouldn't mind helping you out, knowing how much she likes horses."

Sara let out a little sigh. "I suppose she'd do it. I'll ask her tomorrow."

Mom laughed. "How complicated we're making things. If we decide to go to Wyalusing, it'll be for only a week and not for the entire summer." She looked across the table at her husband. "What is this French Azilum you're researching, John?"

Dad's eyes lit up, as they usually did when he discussed a project he was working on. Their father was an historian and taught history at Maplewood College. Each summer he usually took what he called a "field trip" to an historical site he was writing about. Whenever he could, he liked to take his family with him.

Now he leaned back in his chair, a slight smile curving his lips. "French Azilum," he said, savoring the name as if it were something special. "I'm surprised you've never heard of it before, Janice."

Warming up to the subject, he went on, "It was a settlement for refugees of the French Revolution. Because of their loyalty to the king, the émigrés, as the French refugees were called, were forced to flee to America to escape imprisonment and death by the guillotine. When they arrived here in 1793, they gathered in Philadelphia, formed a land company, and bought a large tract of land along the east branch of the Susquehanna River. There they laid out a town with a two-acre market square and 413 lots. By 1794 thirty log houses had been built. It has been said, although the foundations haven't been found as yet, that the émigrés had even built a log mansion for their queen, Marie Antoinette, and her children. It was called La Grand Maison and was supposed to have been one of the largest log houses built in America."

"Did Marie Antoinette and her children actually live in the log mansion?" asked Sara, showing sudden interest in what their father was saying. She couldn't imagine such a glamorous French queen living in a log house in the Pennsylvania wilderness.

"No," Dad said, shaking his head. "Marie Antoinette followed her husband, King Louis XVI, to the guillotine on October 16, 1793."

"What about her children?" Sam asked, leaning forward intently. "Did they escape to America?"

"That's a mystery in history that has never been solved," Professor Harmon replied. "The older son, the Dauphin, became ill and died in France. That we know. I'm not sure what became of his sister, but it is said that the younger son, Louis Charles, died in prison. However, some historians claim that the little prince was smuggled out of his prison cell by the wife of his jailer in a laundry basket of dirty clothes and sent to America disguised as a sickly French girl.

16

Whether he ever lived in Azilum or not was never known. No one claims he did—but who knows?"

"And are you trying to solve that mystery, Dad?" Tim asked.

His father shook his head. "No, I don't believe the mystery can ever be solved. What I'm interested in is writing an article about the restoration that is going on at French Azilum. So little has been written about it, and I think it's an interesting chapter in American history."

"It sure is," Sam said. "I'd like to see the place. I really would."

"So would I," agreed Sara, sharing her brother's enthusiasm.

"Well, I guess that settles it then," Mom said, smiling at her family. "Except for Tim, we'll be spending a week in Wyalusing. When do we leave?"

"I'll call Charles right now and set a date," Dad said. "I know he and Blair will be happy that you're coming."

He half arose from his chair, then sat down again. He smiled, his eyes twinkling. "By the way," he said, directing his attention to Sara and Sam, "Charles wrote that he has been working on a family mystery that he thought I might be interested in. He didn't go into detail, but I believe it has something to do with a lost heirloom. Maybe you two would like to have a try at solving it."

Sam flashed a crooked grin at his sister. "Could be, huh, Twinny?"

Sara nodded eagerly and smiled back.

Although Sara and Sam were twins, with the same auburn hair and hazel eyes, their father often remarked that they were alike in a very different way. Sam was tall and lanky, had a crooked smile, and was called Superbrain by his friends in school. Sara was slightly plump, pretty, and liked people more than she did books. But one thing they always agreed on—they both liked to solve mysteries.

Dad went to the phone in the hallway to make his call. When he returned to the table, he said that Charles and Blair would be happy to have them as soon as they could come.

"Give me a couple of days to get ready," Mom said as she stood up and started to clear the table. "I believe we can leave by the end of the week."

Early the next morning Sara rode her bike down the road to Fox Ridge Farm. As she rode up the lane leading to the Rabers' stable, she noticed Amy's bike propped against the corral fence.

Amy Goodwin lived in town and became Sara's best friend last fall when she helped the twins solve the mystery of the secret code that led to the discovery of a hidden treasure. Amy loved horses as much as Sara, and the two girls had offered to help exercise the riding horses at Fox Ridge Farm this summer.

"Hi!" Sara called out as she entered the stable and found her friend tacking up her favorite horse, Bumper.

Tim and Huy Chau, the Rabers' foster son, were mucking out the stalls, and Amy informed Sara that Vickie was taking some kids from Maplewood on a trail ride.

Sara went to the tack room for Dusty's gear, and after the gentle mare had been bridled and saddled, Sara swung up in the saddle and joined Amy in the corral.

They put their mounts through their paces, working up from a jog to a gallop, then they rode the trail leading across the field and through the woods. While they were walking the horses back to the corral to cool them off, Sara asked Amy if she would be willing to exercise Dusty next week.

"Sure," Amy said. "Where are you going?"

"To a town called Wyalusing in the Endless Mountains," Sara explained.

"Wow, that sounds like out of nowhere," Amy piped. "Where are the Endless Mountains?"

"Not too far away," replied Sara. "Dad said they are in northeastern Pennsylvania. He's going there to do some research for an article he's writing. Anyway, this friend of his who lives in a big house in Wyalusing has invited the whole family to stay with him and his son Blair."

Without hesitation Amy asked with a giggle, "Is Blair cute?"

"How should I know?" Sara laughed. "I haven't even seen the guy yet. Maybe he's just a little kid."

"Doesn't sound that way," Amy quipped with a roll of her eyes.

"Anyway," Sara said, ignoring her friend's gesture, "Dad said that Blair's father mentioned something about a family mystery."

"I might have known!" Amy said, bobbing her head up and down. "Nothing could keep you and Sam away from a good mystery."

"I know," Sara laughed. She reached over in the saddle and gave Dusty a gentle pat. "I keep wondering what it can be. Dad said something about a lost heirloom."

"Hmm," murmured Amy as they led their mounts back into the stable. "A lost heirloom. Sounds interesting."

"I'll write and let you know all about it as soon as we get there," Sara promised.

Amy's cheeks dimpled. "If I know you, Sara Harmon, you won't be writing any letters until you get that mystery solved."

Sara grinned back at her friend. "Could be."

2
The Intruder

AFTER saying good-bye to Tim, who had reassured Mom a dozen times that he'd be okay and that he'd look after things while they were gone, the Harmons drove out of the drive and were on their way.

Dad thought the quickest way to get to the Endless Mountains was to take the Pennsylvania Turnpike north. After they drove through the Blue Mountain Tunnel, the rolling farm country changed to mountain scenery.

"Are these the Endless Mountains?" Sara asked, looking around her at the low, wooded ranges.

"No, these are the Poconos," Mom replied from the front seat. "Open your window and feel how cool the air is now."

"And how unpolluted," Sam added, taking a deep breath.

"We won't reach the Endless Mountains until we leave the city of Scranton," Dad said. And two hours later, after they had turned off on Route 6, they got their first glimpse of the beautiful mountain ranges to the northwest.

"The Endless Mountains are part of the Allegheny plateau," Dad informed them. "From here the Allegheny range runs southwestward across the state to become the Cumberland Mountains in Kentucky." He grinned over his shoulder at the twins. "So much for the geography lesson."

They passed through small towns and villages with strange-sounding Indian names like Tunkhannock and Meshoppen. The road wound along the Susquehanna River until they finally reached Wyalusing.

"What a pleasant little town," Mom remarked as they drove up Main Street where the old storefronts still existed today as they had more than a century ago.

Dad stopped at the post office on Church Street to ask the way to Charles LaRue's house, and soon they were driving up a quiet residential street where tall, shady maples grew at intervals along the sidewalk.

Dad slowed down when they came to a large Victorian frame house that reminded Sara of something out of a mystery tale. As they swung into the driveway that led across a green, sloping lawn, she leaned forward to get a better look at the house.

A long veranda, embellished with white gingerbread trim, ran halfway around it. Four brick chimneys thrust upward from the gray slate roof. There were even two small balconies overlooking a formal garden that rimmed the entire one side of the house.

"Wow!" exclaimed Sam. "Mr. LaRue wasn't kidding when he said he lived in a big house."

The driveway led up to the old carriage porch on the opposite side of the house from the garden. Running down the porch steps to meet them was a stocky youth, about Tim's age. He had a cap of dark curly hair, shining blue eyes, and a turned-up nose.

"Hi," he greeted them. "I'm Blair LaRue. I believe you're the Harmons."

"That's right," Dad said, opening the door to the station wagon and shaking the hand Blair extended to him.

Oh my, Sara thought, sizing up the well-mannered boy. What a gentleman! If Amy were here now to see this she'd flip. Then she thought, I hope Blair's not the stuffy type.

But the good-natured smile that curved the boy's generous mouth upward allayed Sara's fears, and after his first burst of hospitality, he seemed like any other normal boy his age, flustered and not quite knowing what to do next.

A plump, smiling gentleman, who Blair very much resembled, appeared on the porch steps and took over as the welcoming committee, much to his son's relief.

"John!" the man called to Dad.

"Charles!" their father responded, and soon the two men had their arms around each other, like long-lost friends.

Professor Harmon introduced his family, then Blair and his father helped the Harmons with their luggage and showed them their rooms.

Sara was delighted with her room. Blair told her it had once been the sitting room off the bedroom her parents were to occupy. With a thrill of discovery Sara opened a French door that led to one of the small balconies overlooking the garden.

What a lovely flower garden, she thought as she stepped out onto the balcony. It reminded her of an old-fashioned English rose garden with grass paths between the flower beds. In the center of the garden was a stone sundial sur-

22

rounded by stately blue iris.

Blair smiled at her enthusiasm. "Dad and I thought you'd like this room with the little balcony, Sara."

"Oh, I do!" Sara exclaimed, stepping back into the room.

"How about a tour of the rest of the house?" Blair suggested.

Sara glanced over at her suitcase at the foot of the bed. "I haven't unpacked yet," she said, "but I guess that can wait until tonight."

Sam joined them, and Blair led the way down a curving staircase to the downstairs hall which was flanked by his father's study on one side and a parlor on the other.

When Blair led them into the parlor, Sara gasped with delight. It was as though she had been wafted back through time to the late nineteenth century. The room was filled with Victorian rosewood furniture. The long narrow windows, which came down almost to the floor, were dressed with lace curtains. A threadbare but beautiful Turkish rug lay on the wide floorboards, and the walls were covered with faded satin wallpaper. Sconces which once held candles, but were now converted to electric lights, framed the wall.

They walked through the parlor to a dining room, where a thin, quick-moving woman with graying hair and a ready smile was setting the table.

"Abby, I'd like you to meet our guests," Blair said. And to Sara and Sam, "This is Abby McGuire, our indispensable 'gal Friday.'"

The housekeeper gave a little laugh and a fluttery wave of her hand. With a hint of an Irish brogue, she said, "Go on with you, Blair LaRue. Flattery won't get you your dinner any sooner." Turning to Sara and Sam, she smiled and said, "Welcome to Wyalusing, m'dears. We've all been looking forward to your visit here."

23

Remembering her manners, Sara returned, "Thank you, Mrs. McGuire. We've been looking forward to being here, too."

"Well, now, make yourselves at home while I see to the dinner," Abby McGuire said. She gave the last napkin on the table a little pat of approval and hurried out of the room. The savory aroma coming from the kitchen across the hall made Sam hope that dinner wouldn't be long.

Blair led them down the hallway to the study in front of the house where they found Mr. LaRue and Mom and Dad talking. Mr. LaRue arose and gestured the twins to a rosewood settee. Blair sank into a leather chair by his father's desk.

"Mr. LaRue has been telling us that this house is over a hundred years old," Mom said after Sara and Sam settled on the settee. As Sara's eyes scanned the room, she noticed that the study had a French door opening out into the garden, just like the French door in her room upstairs.

"The house was built by Claude LaRue's grandson in 1880," Mr. LaRue told them. "I'm afraid its furnishings are rather gaudy and somewhat outmoded, for it was built during the Victorian period. But I was born here and so was Blair. It's been home to us, and we haven't the least desire to change it."

"It's lovely as it is," Mrs. Harmon assured him. "I wouldn't change a thing."

"I take it that Claude LaRue was an ancestor of yours, Charles," Professor Harmon said.

Their genial host nodded, his eyes twinkling. "I suppose while we wait for dinner, I could tell you about our family history in Wyalusing. It is an interesting one, and it has a mystery that we have never been able to solve."

At the mention of the mystery, the twins sat up with

24

interest. "Does it have something to do with the lost heirloom?" Sam asked, his eagerness showing in his face.

Mr. LaRue settled back in his chair and clasped his pudgy hands across his chest. "Yes, it does, Sam," he replied. "But let me start at the beginning. Our family history in America began with Claude LaRue and his younger brother, Jacques, who came to America just before the French Revolution to seek a better way of life. In order to see more of the American back country, the brothers got work as polemen on the Durham boats that brought supplies from Philadelphia up the Susquehanna River to the early settlements here in the northern part of the state.

"When the French Revolution broke out, many of their countrymen had to flee for their lives. Like Claude and Jacques, many came to America, but even in Philadelphia there was the fear of French revolutionary spies. So in 1793 the émigrés formed a colony here in northern Pennsylvania called Azilum. During those exciting years Claude and Jacques LaRue were kept busy poling the émigrés up the Susquehanna to French Azilum."

Warming up to his story, Mr. LaRue leaned forward in his chair. "It so happened that one of the émigrés who came up the river was a French nobleman whom the brothers had helped escape from spies in Philadelphia. In gratitude for their help, the émigré gave Claude and Jacques identical gold pendants in the shape of a fleur-de-lis. He told the brothers that the pendants had belonged to members of his family who had been guillotined along with other political prisoners in Paris."

Mr. LaRue paused and looked over at the twins. "Do you know what a fleur-de-lis is?" he asked.

Sara shook her head with a puzzled frown. But Sam spoke up, "I believe it's the flower design of the insignia used in

25

heraldry. You know, like on knights' shields."

Mr. LaRue nodded. "That's right, young man. And it was the royal emblem of the French government before the Revolution. It represented the lilies of France, an emblem dear to all Frenchmen. Here in America we call the lilies of France the iris." Mr. LaRue paused with a smile. "You'll find iris growing in most French gardens."

Sara smiled back. "Like in your garden, Mr. LaRue."

Their host nodded and went on with his story.

"The brothers, Claude and Jacques, were very fond of their identical pendants and wore them around their necks on gold chains. Claude wrote in his journal that the fleur-de-lis pendants reminded them of the home they had left across the sea.

"Later in his journal Claude wrote that he and Jacques had saved enough of their earnings to buy land across the river from Azilum. Because America was being settled so rapidly and there was a great demand for lumber in the growing cities, the brothers decided to build a lumber mill in Wyalusing and go into business together. The mill prospered, and Claude married and raised a family on the site of this house. But not all was well. The brothers had a quarrel. Claude did not mention in his journal the cause of the quarrel, but it was bitter enough to separate them. Jacques went off angrily, taking only his fleur-de-lis pendant and his personal belongings. He never returned.

"As the years passed, Claude was saddened by his brother's absence and regretted the argument that had separated them. He searched everywhere for Jacques and even offered a reward for any news concerning his lost brother. But his search was fruitless.

"Before he died, Claude made a will in which half of the earnings from the lumber mill was to be put into a trust fund for Jacques' heirs, wherever they were. Through the years the descendants of Claude LaRue honored his will and the trust grew. They, too, had tried to solve the mystery of what had become of Jacques and his descendants, but without success. And now, in this generation, it is my responsibility to try to solve that mystery and reunite the families of the two brothers—just as Claude would have wanted."

Mr. LaRue paused and his face was somber. "It is a sad thing when brothers quarrel and separate. I would like nothing better than to bring our two families happily together again."

Professor Harmon looked consolingly at his friend. "I realize how you must feel, Charles, but after two centuries, it sounds like an impossible task."

"I know," Mr. LaRue replied, shaking his head, "but I do have a clue—something to go on."

"A clue?" Sam asked, his eyes bright with curiosity.

Their host nodded. "The family heirlooms. The two identical fleur-de-lis pendants," he replied. "Claude's pendant has been handed down from one generation to another, and I'm sure Jacques' family had done the same with his. Claude must have thought so, too, for one of the provisions in his will was that Jacques' heirs must prove themselves by presenting their ancestor's fleur-de-lis pendant in order to claim their inheritance. So, if I could find the matching pendant—the lost heirloom—the mystery would be solved."

He arose from his chair and walked over to his desk. He took a key from his pocket, and unlocked the top drawer and drew out a flat, velvet-covered case. He moved to the open French door where the light was better and opened the case. They gathered around him in a tight circle.

"Oh, my," Mrs. Harmon exclaimed when Mr. LaRue

drew out the pendant. "What a lovely piece of jewelry!"

The twins stared at the three golden petals of the fleur-de-lis. The central petal stood erect, the other two gently curving away from it. They were joined together by a horizontal band below which the ends of the stems were visible. The pendant hung from a gold chain, simple in design, yet elegant.

Mr. LaRue handed the pendant to Professor Harmon, who examined it closely. "I have read about the heirlooms the émigrés brought with them when they fled from France," he said. "They were very fine pieces and only a few are in circulation now. As antique jewelry, this piece must be very valuable."

"In itself, yes," Mr. LaRue agreed, "but its companion

Suddenly Sara glimpsed a man moving stealthily from behind the tree that shaded the French door.

piece is even more valuable to me because it will help me find Jacques' missing heirs."

While they went on discussing the pendant, Sara glanced out at the sunlit garden. The tall stately iris in the center did resemble the fleur-de-lis, she thought. The lilies of France made a lovely emblem.

Suddenly she stiffened. Out of the corner of her eye she glimpsed the figure of a man moving stealthily from behind the big maple tree that shaded the French door. Mystified by his peculiar movements, Sara directed her full attention on the intruder.

He couldn't be a gardener, she thought, because he wasn't dressed like one. He was a tall, thin, middle-aged man with dark hair receding from a high forehead. He had a neatly clipped beard and wore a tan business suit. He was so intent in staring at the fleur-de-lis pendant in her father's hand that he was unaware that he was being observed. Not until he met Sara's staring glance did he look startled.

Sara let out a gasp, and in that moment the man ducked back behind the tree trunk and was gone.

3
The Council Grounds

WHAT'S the matter, Sara?" asked Mrs. Harmon.

They all stopped talking and looked up with surprise when they heard Sara's gasp and saw the shocked look on her face.

"A man!" Sara cried in a quick, breathless voice. She pointed in the direction of the big maple just outside the French door. "I saw a man eavesdropping on us. When he saw that I was watching him, he disappeared behind that tree."

Sam and Blair leaped into action at once and ran out through the French door. Mr. LaRue quickly put the fleur-de-lis pendant back in its case and locked it in the top drawer of his desk. When the boys returned, breathless from their search around the house, Blair announced, "We didn't see anyone."

"We circled the house and even ran out to the street," said Sam, puffing like a steam engine. "He sure did get away fast."

Mr. LaRue shook his head. "It must have been a curious sightseer. The town's full of them this week because of the Indian council at Wyalusing Rocks. It wouldn't be the first time an inquisitive tourist sneaked into our yard to take a look at our old-fashioned house and garden."

Just then Abby McGuire announced dinner, and they let the matter drop. But all through the delicious meal, Sara kept wondering about the intruder. He may have been a curious sightseer, she thought, but he was also a curious eavesdropper, spying on them from behind that tree.

After dinner when the young people were sitting in wicker chairs on the veranda, Sara brought up the subject of the intruder again. And this time she insisted that he was more than just an inquisitive sightseer.

"Maybe it was Ed Conners you saw," Blair mused. "He's a handyman in town who takes care of our lawn and garden. Sometimes the slow way he walks makes him look as if he's sneaking around. And he is nosy."

"Does he wear a tan business suit and have a beard?" asked Sara. The intruder she saw didn't exactly resemble a handyman.

Blair laughed. "Well, hardly. I've never seen him in anything but jeans and an old sweatshirt. And the only beard he has is when he hasn't shaved for a day or two."

"Then he couldn't be Ed Conners," Sara replied firmly. "The man I saw wasn't interested in the garden. He was definitely eavesdropping on us."

"But why should anyone be spying on us?" Blair exclaimed, his deep voice breaking into a protesting squeak. "Dad's no foreign agent or anything." He paused for a moment, then looked at the twins with wide eyes. "Do you suppose he saw the fleur-de-lis pendant and heard what Dad was telling about it?"

Sara nodded. "I'm sure he did."

Sam drew his brows together in a puzzled frown. "But what good would that information do him unless he has the matching pendant?"

"Well, I hope he doesn't, and I hope he never comes around here again," Sara said with a little shiver. "There was something about him I didn't like."

They sat in silence for a minute, then moving on to another subject, Sam asked, "What did your dad mean, Blair, by an Indian council at Wyalusing Rocks?"

"That's what I wanted to talk to you about this evening," Blair said. "You see, all this week the Susquehannock and Tuscarora tribes are holding a Grand Council meeting here at Wyalusing Rocks. According to our newspaper, displays of Indian artifacts, arts and crafts, archery contests, and ceremonial dancing will be open to the public. While your dad is busy with his research over at Azilum, I thought maybe you'd like to take in the events at the council grounds."

"That'd be neat," Sam said. "But just where are the Wyalusing Rocks?"

Blair shook his head. "I forget that you're not from around here. The Wyalusing Rocks are a series of big ledges on a bluff above the river, about two miles north of here. If you had come to Wyalusing from the north along Route 6, instead of up from the south, you would have passed them. Anyway, the Susquehannocks and the Tuscaroras were early Indian tribes who used to live around here. They considered the ledges sacred and called them the Wyalusing Prayer

Rocks. That's why their descendants are holding their council meetings there."

Blair paused with a smile. "Actually, today you wouldn't know that the Susquehannocks and Tuscaroras are native Americans if they weren't in their tribal dress. The newspaper account said that they come from all walks of life. Doctors, lawyers...."

"And Indian chiefs," quipped Sam.

"Yeah," Blair smiled. "But at the Grand Council meeting they forget all that and celebrate the customs of their ancestors."

"I think that's wonderful," Sara spoke up. "I mean, it's really great that they keep alive the old ways of the native Americans."

"A lot of other people must think so, too," Blair answered. "The Grand Council meeting is sure drawing a lot of spectators. Tourists are coming from all over. Anyway, how about going up there tomorrow and taking a look around?"

The twins nodded enthusiastically. "Sounds good to me," Sam agreed.

With her thoughts turned to the Indian council, Sara forgot about the strange man she had seen in the garden that afternoon. It wasn't until she was alone in her room that night and had walked out onto the little balcony and glanced down at the dark garden that she remembered how stealthily their intruder had slipped from behind that maple tree.

She glanced over at the big tree now, half-expecting to see a shadowy form watching her from behind it. But the tree stood dark and quiet, with only a slight breeze moving the tips of its branches.

She closed the French door and slipped into bed. After saying her prayers, she dropped off to a sound sleep and didn't awaken until Sam and Blair pounded on her door the next morning.

"Come on, sleepyhead, get up," they called on their way to breakfast.

Sara dressed in jeans and a blue jersey. Following the sound of voices to the kitchen, she found the boys already eating a hearty breakfast, presided over by Abby McGuire.

The housekeeper told them that Mr. LaRue had taken Professor and Mrs. Harmon over to Azilum early that morning so that the professor could get started on his research. Mrs. Harmon had taken her sketch pad along so that she could sketch the artifacts for her husband.

"They won't be back for lunch," Mrs. McGuire said. "What about you three?"

"We'll grab something at the council grounds," Blair replied. "I hear they have good grilled beefburgers there."

The boys waited for Sara to finish her breakfast. Then the three of them said good-bye to Abby McGuire, and Blair led the way out the back door to the old carriage barn that had been transformed into a garage.

"We won't have to hike up to Wyalusing Rocks," Blair informed them happily. "I just passed my driver's exam, and Dad said I could use the pickup."

He opened the garage door and led the way to a white pickup truck with LARUE LUMBER COMPANY stamped on the door panel. They stepped up into the cab and Blair started the engine. After three unsuccessful attempts, the engine finally roared to life, and they drove out of the garage and down the driveway. When they came to busy Route 6, Blair guided the pickup onto the northbound lane, and after climbing the curving river bluff, they arrived at a turnout where a sign announced Wyalusing Rocks.

Already the parking area at the turnout was filled with

cars. Some of the tourists were taking the narrow path that led along a high cliff to the overhangs of rock while others were crossing the highway making their way to the council grounds.

Sara and Sam were curious about the Prayer Rocks that the Indians held sacred, but Blair said, "Let's take a tour of the council grounds before it gets too crowded."

They followed him across the highway and climbed a winding, grassy lane that led to a clearing at the top of the bluff.

"What a view!" exclaimed Sara as she gazed across at the river valley.

"Wait until you see it from the rocks," Blair told her.

At the entrance to the council grounds they were greeted by a large totem pole with figures of animals and birds carved on its round surface. One dark carving resembled the face of a wolf. Above it was the brown face of a bear with its long snout. And at the very top was the carving of a large black bird with its wings outstretched. As they were studying the carvings, a voice behind them announced: "Wyalusing Totem of Peace."

They swung around to see a teenage boy dressed in a white T-shirt and fringed buckskin pants. But what caught Sara's attention was the beautiful red-and-white-beaded bird design embroidered on his moccasins. His friendly brown eyes smiled at them.

"Welcome to the Grand Council of the Susquehannocks and Tuscaroras," he greeted. "I am a guide, and if you want a tour of the council grounds, I shall be glad to show you around."

"Hey, yeah," Blair said eagerly. "My name's Blair LaRue and these are my friends, Sara and Sam Harmon."

The boy nodded. "My name is Jim Burton, but at the

Grand Council I'm known as Jim Little Hawk. You may call me by my Indian name if you like."

He glanced up at the totem pole, and in a tone that told them he had rehearsed the words many times, he said, "First, let me explain the totem. It is a memorial to the Ancients of Ancients of the Americas and is dedicated to everlasting world peace. On top of the totem is the thunderbird and on the side that faces the Prayer Rocks to the west are symbols of the families and clans that once worshiped here, like the Wolf Clan and the Bear Clan."

"So the totem is like a family tree," Sam spoke up.

Jim Little Hawk nodded. "Yes, but it is more than that. On this side facing the rising sun are carved emblems of the faith of our early religion. They are to remind us of the obligation to pray at sunrise, at noon, and at sunset each day, thanking the Creator for what he has given us. Of course we are all Christians now, but we still offer this prayer three times a day: 'Great Spirit of Spirits, thank you for creating this beautiful day. Thank you for giving this beautiful day to the Children of the Forest and to all men.'"

"What a lovely prayer!" murmured Sara as they turned from the totem and followed Jim Little Hawk into the council grounds.

The open grassy field at the top of the bluff was filled with native Americans in Indian dress and sightseers who were milling around the half-dozen log cabins where Indian crafts were displayed and souvenirs were sold.

Sam pointed to a long rectangular structure that stood in the center of the field. It was covered with long sheets of bark and had a curved roof like a Quonset hut. "What is that building?" he asked.

"That is a Susquehannock longhouse," Jim Little Hawk informed them. "In the old days several families of the same

36

lineage would live there. Now it is used as the council house where the chiefs and head women hold their council meetings. The leaders of the Grand Council are Chief Sun Bear and Princess Morning Star, who are Susquehannocks. The other chiefs are from the Tuscarora Reserve in New York State. They meet in the longhouse to revive the old ways, to commune with the Master of Life, and to counsel with their brothers and sisters."

He paused and added proudly, "Chief Sun Bear is my father."

"Then you are a Susquehannock," Sara said.

The boy nodded. "Yes, I'm Jim Little Hawk of the Susquehannock tribe."

As they walked through the council grounds, Jim Little Hawk paused now and then to point out the different craft cabins. At one cabin, where bunches of dried herbs hung from the roof poles, he explained, "Here was once the wigwam and herb garden of Kwas-sa Koh-wa-nus, Medicine Woman of Field and Forest. It is said that she could cure any illness with her herbs."

They passed the cabin and came to the far end of the council grounds where a line of campers and travel trailers were parked.

"This is where the members of the Grand Council are staying," Jim Little Hawk told them. He pointed to a travel trailer at the far end of the line. "That is my family's trailer."

"You're camped right by the woods," Sam observed.

Jim smiled. "Yeah, it's pretty neat camping out. There's a trail through the woods in back of our trailer." He paused, a sudden eagerness showing in his face. "Would you like to walk back there to see Spirit Lake?"

"What's Spirit Lake?" Sara asked curiously. "Is it part of the council grounds?"

37

Jim Little Hawk nodded. "Yes, in a way it is. There is a legend among my people that on moonlit nights the spirit of an ancient medicine man can be seen rising out of the waters."

"Wow, that sounds spooky," laughed Blair. "You really don't believe that, do you?"

Jim shrugged. "It is only a legend," he replied, "and most sightseers are not interested in our legends. They would rather see our crafts and dances, so we don't usually take them back there. But if you are interested, I'll show it to you."

"Oh, yes," Sara said. "I'd like to see Spirit Lake. Wouldn't you, Sam?"

Her twin nodded with a slight smile twitching the corners of his lips.

They followed Jim Little Hawk past the line of travel trailers and campers to the narrow trail that led through the woods. The trail came out at a large pond surrounded by dark green hemlocks. Here, away from the noise and confusion of the council grounds, it was so quiet that not even a bird sang.

"In the old days Spirit Lake was said to have been much larger than it is now," Jim explained. "But reeds and moss have shrunk its banks until now it's no larger than a big pond."

Sara sank down on a log bench along the edge of the water and looked around her. No wonder it was called Spirit Lake, she thought. The shadowy hemlocks gave the water a smooth, ebony appearance that made it look deep and eerie. Reflections shivered on its dark surface. There was something ethereal about this silent place. Sara could well understand how the early native Americans could imagine a spirit rising out of these dark waters on moonlit nights.

"You can take part in the archery contest," Little Jim Hawk said. "Would you like to try it?"

She glanced around the pond at the deep-green shoreline ringed with woods. Suddenly she caught her breath. Was there something white shimmering through those dark layers of hemlock, she wondered. She squinted so that she could get a better look.

For a full minute she sat there staring at the trees. A ghost perhaps? She laughed at herself and being curious she got up to explore.

When she had walked around the pond to where she had seen the flash of white, she found herself in a small clearing. And there in the middle of it stood a white travel trailer, still attached to the pickup that pulled it. No one seemed to be around, and Sara wondered how the truck and trailer got way back here. Then she noticed the tire marks through the

39

tall grass that led to a narrow graveled road which was hardly more than a trail through the woods.

"Someone's camped here," she called out excitedly to the boys.

They hurried around the pond to where she was standing. Jim Little Hawk stared at the trailer.

"This wasn't here yesterday," he said, puzzled. "I don't know who'd want to camp way back here by themselves."

"Maybe it's one of your council members who just arrived and wants to be alone with nature," Sam suggested. He looked around at the quiet pond and deep woods. "I can't think of a more isolated place to camp."

"Well, if he wants to be alone, we better not bother him," Sara said. "Let's go back to the council grounds. I'd like to see some more of the crafts and exhibits."

Jim gave the travel trailer one more puzzled look, then led the way back through the woods.

When they returned to the council grounds, they found a gathering of men and boys in an open space in back of the longhouse. They were holding bows and arrows and were waiting for a guide to hang a bear's paw target to a tree.

Jim turned to them, his eyes bright with enthusiasm. "You can take part in the archery contest. Would you like to try it?"

"Sure," Blair replied eagerly.

Sara squinted toward the group. "I don't see any women or girls," she said.

"That doesn't matter," Jim told her. "Anyone who wants to can try to hit the bear's paw."

Sara shook her head. "You guys go ahead. I'll browse around the craft cabins while I wait for you."

Sam, who had never shot a bow and arrow in his life, looked ruefully at his twin. "I have a feeling I won't be long in the contest. I don't think I could hit the side of a barn with a bow and arrow."

Jim Little Hawk overheard the remark and replied, "You may be surprised, Sam. There are a lot of amateurs who don't realize how good they are until they try." And with an encouraging pat on Sam's back, he led the way to the open space.

Sara smiled wryly as she watched them go. Although Sam was a brain, he was clumsy in most physical endeavors. She could probably hit the target much better than he. Poor Sam!

She turned and made her way to the craft cabins. In one cabin she spied a woman weaving a basket out of sweet grass. Sara stood behind a small knot of tourists and watched for a while, then she wandered to another cabin where an Indian girl with an awl was doing beadwork on a leather headband.

What beautiful designs she was embroidering, Sara thought. They were the Indian designs of flowers and birds and animals, all done with tiny brightly colored beads that reminded Sara of the bird design on Jim Little Hawk's beaded moccasins.

Several finished bands were for sale, and Sara couldn't resist one with a horse embroidered with white beads. She decided it would be the perfect gift for Amy for taking care of Dusty while she was away.

After she had paid for the headband, Sara made her way to a cabin where turquoise jewelry was displayed. A young Indian woman stood behind the jewelry display. She was wearing a ceremonial dress of beautiful white doeskin, fringed at the hem and designed in red and brown beadwork. She was talking with a tall, thin man. Sara couldn't help admiring the pretty woman. A yoke of long fringe hung

41

down from her shoulders and a beaded headband with two eagle feathers held back her long, dark hair which accented the proud tilt of her head.

The man's back was turned to Sara and he seemed to be doing most of the talking. The Indian woman only shook her head from time to time. As Sara drew closer to look at the turquoise rings, bracelets, and necklaces, she couldn't help overhearing what the man was saying. It seemed that he was trying to buy an item of jewelry that the Indian woman didn't want to sell. She kept shaking her head again and again at his persistent plea.

Finally the man gave up and turned to walk away. He didn't bother to look at Sara, but when she glimpsed his face, she caught her breath. He had a neatly clipped beard and dark hair receding from a high forehead. He wasn't wearing the tan business suit today, but Sara recognized him at once as the same man who had been eavesdropping on them in Mr. LaRue's garden.

She waited for the man to leave the craft cabin, then she approached the Indian woman who was now rearranging some of the jewelry. The woman looked up at her with a smile.

"May I help you?" she asked.

"Oh—yes," Sara said flustered. Then she blurted out, "Who was that man who was talking to you just now?"

The woman seemed surprised at Sara's question. "I don't know," she replied. "A tourist, I suppose, and a persistent one at that. He wanted to buy this pendant I am wearing instead of the turquoise jewelry for sale."

Sara's eyes flew to the brightly colored beads that hung around the woman's neck. Then for a second time she caught her breath. From among the strands of beads, the woman was holding out a pendant for her to see, an ornament of three golden petals that hung from a single gold chain.

Sara's eyes were fairly popping as she gaped at the pendant. It was exactly like the one Mr. LaRue was searching for. The pendant he called the fleur-de-lis!

4
The Missing Pendant

IT must be Jacques' pendant," Sara told Mr. LaRue that night at dinner. "It looked just like the pendant you showed us, so it must be the lost heirloom."

"And who is this Indian woman who was wearing it?" Mr. LaRue asked, catching the bright excitement in Sara's eyes.

"Jim Little Hawk said her name is Princess Morning Star," Sara explained. "She is one of the head women at the Indian council."

"She's a Susquehannock," Blair put in. "Long ago her tribe used to live around here."

"But how did she get Jacques' pendant?" Mr. LaRue asked.

He looked at the vacant expressions around him with a thoughtful expression. Suddenly he seemed to come to a decision. He crumpled his napkin and sat up abruptly. "If you are sure this woman has the matching fleur-de-lis pendant, Sara, then I must see her at once."

Professor Harmon looked across the table at his friend. "Is there any way I can help?" he offered.

"No-no, thank you," Mr. LaRue said. "I know you have your notes of today to sort through, John, and I wouldn't want to interrupt your research." He glanced over at Mrs. Harmon. "But Janice may like to see the council grounds."

"I certainly would," she said smiling. "Why don't we skip dessert so that we can get an earlier start." Noticing the disappointed look on Sam's face, she added, "We can have it after we get back."

"Good idea," said Mr. LaRue, pushing his chair away from the table. "We'll leave right now if you're ready."

A few minutes later they were in his car, heading up the road to the Prayer Rocks. When they reached the council grounds, they found it deserted. The tourists that had crowded the grounds that day were gone, and all the craft cabins were closed. No one seemed to be around.

Bewildered, Sara stared at the empty grounds. "I have no idea where we can find Princess Morning Star if she's not at her craft cabin."

Just then Sam noticed a thin line of smoke rising from behind the longhouse. He motioned them to follow him to the open space where several boys were sitting around a campfire on sleeping bags.

One of the boys leaped to his feet when he saw them and hurried in their direction.

Sam called out, "Hi," when he recognized their friendly guide, Jim Little Hawk.

"Hi," Jim returned. He seemed surprised to see them. "The crafts and exhibits are all closed, Sam. I'm sorry, but there's nothing scheduled tonight for the tourists."

Sam suddenly felt as though they were intruding into the private lives of the council members. But Blair and his father looked so intent that he hastily explained, "The reason we're here is that Blair's father wants to speak with Princess Morning Star. It's about something very important."

Mr. LaRue stepped forward. "I promise I won't disturb her long, young man. Could you please tell her that Charles LaRue is here and would like to speak to her for a moment?"

Jim nodded and was off on his errand. He soon returned, slightly breathless from hurrying. "She says she'll see you. Come with me."

He led the way to the line of trailers at the back of the council grounds. He stepped in front of one of the larger trailers and knocked on the door. Immediately it was opened by a young woman dressed in a pullover sweater and slacks, a frilly apron around her waist.

At first glance Sara hardly recognized the Indian princess without her ceremonial dress and feathered headband. Now she looked just like any other ordinary young housewife— which she was, they soon discovered, when she introduced them to a smiling young man who came to stand by her side.

"This is my husband, David Greenleaf," she told them.

The young couple invited Jim and their guests into the trailer. Sara sat down next to her mother on a cushioned bench and looked around her at the cozy interior. Bright yellow curtains hung at the windows. The kitchen, complete with cupboards, a small stove and refrigerator, and a foldaway table, blended in nicely with the rest of the living area. Mr. LaRue joined his host and hostess at the little table and the boys squatted on cushions on the floor.

46

"You have a cozy trailer here," Mrs. Harmon said pleasantly. "It's just like a little home."

"It is home," David Greenleaf replied. "You see, we travel around a lot and have to take our home with us."

"We do mission work on reservations all around the country," Princess Morning Star explained. Glancing fondly at her husband, she went on, "David is an ordained minister, and I help him bring the Word of God to those who are less fortunate than we. We took time out of our busy schedule to come here to the Grand Council meeting so that I could meet with members of my ancestral tribe."

"You could call it a vacation," her husband put in quickly. "It is good to be back East again in the beautiful Endless Mountains."

"Then I take it you do most of your work in the West?" inquired Mr. LaRue.

David nodded. "Yes, right now we are helping our Navajo brothers and sisters in Arizona."

"Is that where you got all that beautiful turquoise jewelry?" Sara asked, recalling the pounded silver and turquoise rings, bracelets, and necklaces she had seen at the craft cabin.

The young woman nodded. "We are selling the Navajo jewelry to get money for the reservation. There is still much hardship and poverty on many of the reservations."

Everyone was silent for a moment, then Princess Morning Star asked Mr. LaRue, "What is it you wanted to talk to me about? If I can help you in any way, I'd be glad to."

Mr. LaRue cleared his throat and said, "It's about the fleur-de-lis pendant Sara told me you were wearing today."

Princess Morning Star's hand went automatically to her throat. "My gold pendant?" she asked, puzzled.

"The one the tourist wanted to buy," Sara reminded her.

47

"Oh, yes," Princess Morning Star said, her face brightening. "He was persistent, I remember."

"Would you mind showing us the pendant?" Mr. LaRue broke in eagerly.

"I'll be glad to," Princess Morning Star replied. "I took it off and put it in my jewel box with my ceremonial beads. But why do you wish to see it?"

Mr. LaRue sat forward and interlaced the fingers of his hands. "I know I owe you an explanation of why I am so eager to see it, but first, will you tell me where you got it?"

"Of course," Princess Morning Star replied. "I am an only child. My parents both died quite young. When my mother knew that she had an incurable illness and would not have long to live, she gave me the pendant and told me to treasure it because it had been in her family a long time. She told me the pendant belonged to one of our ancestors, a Frenchman, who had left his home to live with our people. He had married one of our women and went west with the Susquehannocks when they left this area. Before our French ancestor died, he had presented his son with the beautiful gold pendant and told him to keep it in the family as a remembrance of the country his father had come from. He called the pendant the fleur-de-lis, the lilies of France."

The twins and Blair looked at one another with excitement. The fleur-de-lis pendant Princess Morning Star was talking about must be the lost heirloom, the pendant belonging to Jacques LaRue!

Mr. LaRue's eyes sparkled with lively interest as he, in turn, told Princess Morning Star about the two brothers, how they had quarreled, and how Jacques had left with only his personal belongings and the fleur-de-lis pendant. He told how all these years his family had been searching for Jacques' descendants so that old grievances could be resolved and the LaRue family could be whole and happy again. "I know that both Claude and Jacques would have wanted it that way," he said.

When he finished, Princess Morning Star murmured, "It is a strange and sad story about those two brothers. Brothers should always love one another. We have been taught that as little children."

"And forgiving and being forgiven is the Christian way," David Greenleaf reminded them.

Princess Morning Star got up quickly from the bench by the table. "I will get the fleur-de-lis pendant and we shall see. When I am not wearing it, I keep it in my jewel box."

"And I have brought mine along, too," said Mr. LaRue, taking the flat jewel case from the pocket of his jacket. "We can compare them." His voice rose in anticipation. "From what you have told us, I am sure they will be alike and you are Jacques' long lost heir."

Their eager eyes followed Princess Morning Star as she opened a small closet door at the end of the trailer. From the top shelf she drew out a jewel box. For a long while she seemed to be examining the contents of the box.

Sara's heart thumped in her throat while they waited to see the pendant. Why was Princess Morning Star lingering so long over her jewelry, she wondered.

It seemed ages until the young woman replaced the box on the closet shelf and shut the door. Slowly she turned to face her guests. Sara's eyes darted down to her empty hands and then flew up to her pale face.

"The fleur-de-lis—" The Indian princess spoke in a puzzled voice. "The pendant—is gone!"

5

Voices at the Prayer Rocks

ON the drive back to Wyalusing, Blair discussed develop-
ments with his father. "Princess Morning Star
must be Jacques LaRue's descendant, Dad. I mean, the way
she described the fleur-de-lis pendant and how it got into
her family and all."

"Yes, I believe her," Mr. LaRue said gravely. "But
Claude specified in his will that Jacques' heirs must prove
themselves by presenting their ancestor's fleur-de-lis pendant in order to claim the inheritance. Regretfully, Princess
Morning Star could not do that."

"I wonder what happened to her pendant?" Sara said
thoughtfully. "She was wearing it with her ceremonial beads
today. I know she was because I saw it and so did that man

who was trying to buy it, the same man who was eavesdropping on us."

Sam's eyebrows shot up. "Do you think he could have wanted it so badly that he stole it?"

Their mother cut in, "Princess Morning Star didn't seem to think so. She said it wasn't the first time a tourist had wanted to purchase the pendant. And she was certain that she was wearing it when she changed from her ceremonial dress to her slacks and sweater."

"I know," Sara said with a sigh. "She said she always put it away in her jewel box with her beads."

"Well, maybe this time she just thought she put it in her jewel box," Blair reasoned. "She, herself, began to wonder if she may have mislaid it."

Mr. LaRue shook his head doubtfully. "You don't go around mislaying heirlooms that are dear to you, and I don't believe Princess Morning Star did, either."

Seeing the troubled looks on the faces around her, Mrs. Harmon said consolingly, "Well, cheer up. She'll probably find it."

"I hope so," Blair said. "It'd sure be neat to have an Indian princess in our family."

"By the way," his father spoke up, "just before we left, David Greenleaf asked me if we'd all like to come to church at the council grounds tomorrow."

Sara gave a little squeal of delight. "Oh, yes."

Mr. LaRue glanced through the rearview mirror at her and smiled. "I thought you'd like that, Sara, so I told him we'd be there."

The next morning the Harmons and LaRues, along with several other non-Indian families, gathered with the council members in the outdoor chapel near the peace totem. They sat on split log benches before an altar made of flat stones.

51

David Greenleaf, the pastor, opened the service by reading a familiar verse in Psalms: "The heavens declare the glory of God; and the firmament showeth his handywork."

He then talked about the wonders of God that they could see all around them: the beautiful river below, the wall of mountains beyond, and the blue dome of sky above with its moving cloud frescoes. He talked about brotherhood and how God, the Great Spirit, had sent his Son to earth to bring that love for one's brother to all people.

When his sermon was finished, the Indian congregation sang a hymn in their native language. Then Princess Morning Star gave a message for her people and their visitors. She explained that even though they worship God now, they also keep the old ways, like teaching the children about their Earth Mother through crafts, songs, and stories.

"Mother Earth is good to us, giving us rivers and forests, green fields and mountains. We should always treat her kindly," she explained. Another hymn was sung, then the service ended.

Before they left the chapel, Jim Little Hawk made his way through the gathering to where they stood, admiring the view before them.

"I am glad you are here," he said, beaming. "You see, we are Christians, too.

"And today I believe we all have become a little part Indian," Mrs. Harmon told him. "The service was beautiful. I have never realized just how wonderful our Mother Earth is and how so often we have ignored her."

"Spoken like a true native American," said the tall, dignified man by Jim's side. He smiled, and his dark eyes sparkled. He was dressed in a long-sleeved, fringed ceremonial tunic that hung down over fringed leggings. An impressionistic design of the sun was embroidered in beadwork

52

on the front of his tunic and a full headdress of eagle feathers flowed over his shoulders.

Jim turned to the man. "I would like you to meet my father, Chief Sun Bear," he said proudly.

Sara and Sam were thrilled to be shaking hands with a real Indian chief.

Chief Sun Bear smiled and said, "I am an accountant living in Tamaqua, Pennsylvania. My other name is Gerald Burton." At the surprised look on Sara's face, he added, "I hope that doesn't disappoint you too much, young lady."

"Oh-oh, no, Mr. Burton—not if we can call you Chief Sun Bear here at the Grand Council."

"I would like that very much because, you see, that is my real Indian name."

While their parents talked with Chief Sun Bear, Blair suggested that they take a look at the Prayer Rocks. Jim accompanied them out of the council grounds and down the winding lane which led to the highway. On the other side they walked across the turnout and took a narrow but well-worn path that led along the edge of the river bluff to the rocks.

They passed two small overhangs, and not far beyond they came to a cluster of wide ledges that thrust outward over the steep wooded cliff. They walked across several flat rocks and took a long step downward onto the largest ledge.

"Be careful and don't walk out too far," Blair warned. "There's a drop of 500 feet to the river."

Sara and Sam caught their breath at the view below and beyond them. At the foot of the steep bluff was the curving Susquehanna, and across the river, laid out like a patchwork quilt, stretched a beautiful green plain of fields and meadows. The blue ridges of the Endless Mountains shimmered beyond the plain to the west.

Sam stepped farther out on the overhang and looked

down. "The canoes on the river look like miniature boats," he observed.

"The Susquehanna is good for canoeing," Blair said. "I keep my canoe at the boat landing up the river. One day I'll take you all for a ride."

Sam took another step forward, and Sara reached out to pull him back. "Don't go out so far," she scolded.

Sam drew back and asked, "Why are these ledges called Prayer Rocks by your people, Jim?"

The young Indian guide must have been asked this question many times by sightseers for he had a ready answer. "Because this is sacred land, the place above the beautiful waters where our ancestors heard the voice of the Thunderer, the Great Spirit, and where they saw the Great Light. Many of our famous ancestors have worshiped here, such as Hiawatha, Pontiac, Teedyuscung, Tecumseh, and Red Jacket. The rocks also served as a lookout in the old days. From here my people could see anyone coming up and down the river."

"They sure could," Sam agreed. "Look how far you can see. From one bend in the river to the other."

"By the way," Jim added, "the view from these rocks inspired Charles Wakefield Cadman to compose the Indian song, 'In the Land of the Sky Blue Water.' "

"The river does reflect the sky," Sara said. "It's so beautiful and peaceful."

Blair, who had been squatting on his heels, got up and pointed to the next large ledge. "There's a rock shelter under there. Come on, I'll show you."

He led the way down a short, steep incline and into the dark recess of the neighboring ledge.

As soon as Sara stepped into the shelter, she cried with delight, "It's like a little cave under here. And look, there's a

They could hear the footsteps come to a halt directly overhead as the two men paused on the ledge above them.

rock that is shaped just like a seat." As she settled herself on the rocky protrusion at the back of the shelter, she said, "I feel like a queen on a throne. I think I'll call this rock shelter the throne room."

Sam grinned at Blair and Jim. "Don't mind my goofy sister. She has a wild imagination."

Sara made a face at her twin and settled back more comfortably on her stone throne. The boys sat in crouched positions on the stony floor and for a while they admired the view through the treetops.

Finally Blair arose and said, "Well, I guess we better start back or our folks will wonder what became of us."

While the boys brushed off their good Sunday trousers, Sara slipped off the stone seat and was about to step out from under the rock shelter when suddenly she drew back into the shadows again. At the same instant they heard the crunch of gravel as footsteps sounded on the stony path above them.

"Who's up there?" Blair asked with surprise.

Sara put a finger across her lips. Her face had a pale, surprised look on it. "It's the eavesdropper I saw spying on us at your house, Blair," she whispered, "and there's another man with him."

"That guy sure gets around," Blair muttered.

Now they could hear the footsteps come to a halt directly overhead as the two men paused on the ledge above them. They were talking in low voices. Underneath the thick rock the young people could make out only a mumble of meaningless words at first. But by straining their ears, they were able to catch a fragment of the conversation.

"It's best the two of us aren't seen together. You know where to find me if you need me?" said the voice which Sara recognized as belonging to the man who had tried to buy Princess Morning Star's pendant.

"Sure, Mr. Cheney," replied the other voice, a low gruff one. "At the Lookout."

The two men stopped talking and started to walk away.

After a breathless moment Sam whispered, "Let's follow them to the turnout. I'd like to get a look at them."

They gave the men about a minute's start, then they clambered out from underneath the rock shelter and made their way along the path past the other ledges to the turnout.

At once Sara spied the two men standing by a gray van. They were still so intent on their conversation that they weren't aware of the four young people who were furtively watching them and at the same time pretending to admire the view of the river.

"That tall, thin man with the beard is the one I saw spy-

56

ing on us when Blair's father was telling about Claude's fleur-de-lis pendant," Sara said through narrow lips. "And he was the same man who was trying to buy the pendant from Princess Morning Star. I recognized his voice, too. He must be Mr. Cheney."

His companion was a thick-set, swarthy man with a beaked nose and hooded eyes. He wore a plaid shirt, a pair of fringed deerskin trousers, and beaded moccasins.

Turning to Jim, Sam remarked, "The other guy looks like a council member. Do you know him?"

The Indian boy frowned and shook his head. "No. But I don't know everyone at the council. I'll ask around, though, and see if I can find out who he is."

Finally Mr. Cheney got into the gray van and drove off. His companion crossed the highway and started up the lane to the council grounds.

As Sam watched them leave, he said, "I wonder what they meant by the Lookout."

Blair blinked his eyes thoughtfully and gazed off into space. "There's only one Lookout I know of around here and that's the Marie Antoinette Lookout up the road about five miles. From there you can look directly across the river to the site of French Azilum. There's a little restaurant there, too, and a gift shop and some guest cottages for tourists."

"Then that must be where Mr. Cheney is staying," Sara surmised. "In one of the guest cottages."

"I wish we could have heard everything those two were talking about back at the Rocks," Jim muttered.

"Yeah," Sam agreed with a thoughtful frown. "I wonder why Mr. Cheney doesn't want him and his friend to be seen together." With a puzzled shake of his head, he added, "They sure acted suspicious—as if they're up to something."

6
French Azilum

PROFESSOR Harmon leaned back from the dinner table and breathed a contented sigh. "Mrs. McGuire, that was one of the best Sunday dinners I ever ate," he said with a twinkle in his eye.

The housekeeper blushed with pleasure as she took his empty plate from the table. "Oh, go on with you, Professor. 'Twas just a good Irish pot roast. But thank you just the same."

After dinner the young people were at a loss what to do. "How about a ride over to Azilum and I'll show you around?" Professor Harmon suggested.

"Hey, that's a neat idea," Blair said with alacrity. "We can have a picnic supper at the new pavilion there."

Abby McGuire offered to pack them a lunch, but they shooed her out of the kitchen and got busy themselves, assembly-line fashion. Soon they had assembled a stack of cold roast beef sandwiches, fruit, and a dozen of Mrs. McGuire's homemade cupcakes. With their loaded picnic basket, they got into the station wagon and set out for the old French settlement across the river.

They crossed the Susquehanna on a bridge at the southern end of town and took a macadam road that curved northward along the river. It was a beautiful ride with the shade of a wooded bluff on the one side and the winding river with its many picturesque islands on the other.

Then the road veered away from the river and wound through fields and woodlands. At the tiny village of Durell, they followed the French Azilum signs until they came to a pond alongside the road. Here they turned right on a secondary road that led down to the river again.

At a fork in the road they passed a cluster of houses which Professor Harmon said was Frenchtown. Finally, the road dwindled into a graveled lane, shadowed by a wooded promontory on one side and the curving river on the other.

"Wherever are we going, John?" Mrs. Harmon asked as she glanced down the lonely road. "This is not the way to French Azilum."

"First I'd like to find Homet's Ferry," Professor Harmon said. "I was told it's up this road. You might say it's part of French Azilum because an émigré, Charles Homet, settled here with his family."

He slowed down to study both sides of the road carefully. "There's an interesting story about the Homets," he continued. "Back in France Madame Homet was a waiting maid to Queen Marie Antoinette, and that put her and her family in danger from the revolutionists. Somehow she escaped to America, and it is said that her husband, Charles, swam five miles to a waiting ship that brought him here, too. They lived in Azilum and remained here after most of the other émigrés left."

Mr. LaRue nodded knowingly and added to the story. "Charles Homet built a gristmill on this side of the river and had a ferry so that the farmers across the river could get their grain to his mill. The flats across the river are still known as Homet's Ferry, but there's just a cluster of farms and summer cottages there now. The old mill and the ferry are gone and only the landings on both sides of the river remain."

As they drove on, they passed an abandoned farmhouse with a slanting roof and a porch that looked as if it could collapse at any moment. What a spooky-looking house, Sara thought as she glanced up at the dark empty windows. A drooping hemlock alongside it gave it a mournful look, as if it had been lonely and deserted for a long time.

Beyond the old farmhouse Professor Harmon drew up to a grassy semicircle near the river and parked the station wagon. They all got out and followed him back along the road several yards to a wide stone wall built into the promontory.

"This must be the place where the mill stood," he said, pointing to the wall.

Sara thought it did resemble the side of a large building, perhaps what was left of the old mill. In the center of the wall was implanted a commemorative millstone, inscribed with the words: Site of Homet Mill. Erected 1827.

Blair whistled softly through his lips. "I often paddled my canoe over to the old ferry landing, but I never knew this was here. Come on, I'll show you the landing."

They retraced their steps along the narrow road that curved down to a wide landing of flat rock and hard-packed clay. Beyond the landing was the mouth of a little inlet that opened out onto the broad river.

The inlet was guarded by a rocky spit of land that formed a narrow shoal. At the very end of the stony point, surveying the wide bend in the river below, stood a great blue heron on stilted legs. When it saw them, it gave a low-pitched croak and sailed off on wide wings to the trees along the shore.

As they walked out on the landing, Mr. LaRue said, "This was once the ferry landing. Now it is used as a boat landing for local fishermen."

"The fishing must be pretty good if that heron hangs around here," Sam commented.

"It's so quiet," Mrs. Harmon murmured. "You can even hear the ripples of the eddy at the end of the shoal. They have the sound of a little waterfall."

Sara looked at the ripples of swirling water that curved out from the shoal and disappeared into the smooth deep water at the bend of the river. Except for the small cluster of summer cottages on the far shore, Homet's Ferry was a quiet place, and lonely, too, with only the ghosts of a stone wall and a deserted landing to remind the passersby that a mill and a ferry had once been here.

A little chill crept over Sara as she stood looking out at the river. Deep inside her was the feeling that this wouldn't be the only time she would be standing here on this deserted landing, that sometime soon, for a reason unknown to her now, she would be returning to Homet's Ferry.

She shook off the feeling as the product of her active imagination at work again, but she was glad when they returned to the station wagon and were driving back to where the road came out to sunny green fields and cheerful-looking farmhouses.

When they arrived back at the fork, they chose the road to the right and got their first view of French Azilum, a wide plain in the horseshoe bend of the Susquehanna, the site of the old French village.

They passed several houses and a white colonial church with a pointed spire. Professor Harmon explained that this was the southern edge of Azilum. Some descendants of the émigrés had settled here, and thus it was called Frenchtown.

Beyond the church, in the middle of the horseshoe bend, Professor Harmon pointed out a large boulder with a bronze plaque on it. "This boulder marks the old marketplace and the center of Azilum," he told them. "It was erected by the descendants of the émigrés in memory of their ancestors who remained here."

They followed a road called Queen's Road a short distance to the Gate House where they parked. Before them, bounded by gray stone walls, were four log buildings and a large white house with green shutters.

After they had paid their admission at the Gate House, Professor Harmon explained, with a wave of his arm, "This section of the old town is being restored by the Pennsylvania Historical and Museum Commission. It's said to be the site of the Queen's House. But none of the original buildings of the old French settlement remain. The few log houses here have been reconstructed to resemble the early dwellings of the French émigrés."

He pointed to the largest log building on the site. "That is the reconstructed Du Petit-Thouars log house. It is the museum. We'll go there first."

On the way to the museum they passed a small excavation lined with gray stone walls. "This was once a cellar of one of the log houses," Professor Harmon told them. "The stone walls and the doorway, with two of the original steps leading down, are in excellent condition. This was the first step in excavating the original village sites, and many of the artifacts found here in this cellar site are on display in the museum. Come along and you can see them."

They followed him into the Du Petit-Thouars house where relics found in the old village were displayed in glass cases along the walls. Mrs. Harmon marveled over the lovely French lace and clothing that had belonged to the Azilum women. Mr. LaRue and Blair were fascinated with the steering rudder from a Durham Boat, perhaps like the one Claude and Jacques LaRue manned when bringing émigrés up the Susquehanna. Sara and Sam were interested in the diorama of the original town that stood by the large stone fireplace at the far end of the museum.

The streets and building lots were geometrically designed with the marketplace in the center. Below the marketplace, at the river's edge, were a ferry and a landing.

Professor Harmon joined the twins and pointed to lot 418, north of the marketplace. "This is where we are now, where it is said the Queen's House stood."

"What happened to it and all the other houses?" Sam wondered.

"Azilum lasted only ten years, from 1793 to 1803," their father explained. "The émigrés left the settlement after the Reign of Terror ended in France. Some of them returned to their homeland, and most of the ones who remained in America preferred the southern cities of Charleston, Savannah, and New Orleans, where many other French expatriates lived. So the empty houses here decayed and the chimneys tumbled down. However," their father continued, "a few families other than the Homets remained at Azilum. They were the LaPortes, Lefevres, D'Autremonts, and Brevosts. Their descendants are still living in this area."

When they left the museum, Professor Harmon led the way to the two log houses next to it. In one small cabin dye-making was described. In the other one antique saws, hammers, ice tongs, and old irons were displayed. Across the way was the spinning and weaving cabin with wool and flax wheels, a wool binder, and a 1795 carpet loom.

"How difficult it must have been to have made a dress in those days," Mrs. Harmon remarked as she looked at the balky equipment. "First you had to spin the wool or flax. Then you had to weave it into cloth on a loom before you even began sewing it." She drew in a long sigh. "Just thinking about it makes me weary."

"I'm glad I live now," Sara agreed as they turned away from the spinning and weaving cabin. Beyond a stretch of lawn stood the large white house with the green shutters.

"This is the John LaPorte House," Professor Harmon explained as they waited on the porch for the tour inside. "Because the foundations of the Queen's House have never been found, some historians speculate that this house was built over it. You see, John's father, Barthélomé LaPorte, was an administrator of the French colony. It was said that he and his family lived in the Queen's House after the émigrés left Azilum. It was thought that his son, John, had the Great House torn down because it had become a fire hazard, and this house was built on its site."

Sara looked up at the two white columns that supported the roof of the small square porch. She looked down across the sweeping green lawn to the beautiful river and the tall mountain across from it. A little thrill went through her at the thought that she was standing on what may have been the site of a home built in the wilderness for a queen.

Finally a guide appeared at the front door and announced that this would be the last tour before closing. She showed them through the lovely spacious rooms of the nineteenth-century home and said they could stop at the blacksmith shop and the barn in back of the house where antique farm machinery was displayed.

After they had seen everything, Mr. LaRue glanced at his watch. "We had better head for the pavilion," he said.

"Yeah," Sam agreed heartily. "My stomach tells me it's time for supper."

"Starved as usual," quipped Sara. "Sam eats twice as much as I and never gains a pound," she complained to Blair.

"I don't think that's fair, Sam," Blair teased.

They walked to the front of the LaPorte House, where Professor Harmon pointed out the original iron bell that hung at the ferry landing just below the marketplace. On their way to the pavilion, which was north of the Gate House, he suggested that they detour across the lawn to see the island in the river.

"What's so important about the island, John?" Mrs. Harmon asked.

"It used to be a favorite picnic place for the French ladies, Janice. I thought you might like to see it."

They walked down the long, sloping lawn to the high riverbank. Across a narrow channel was a long island covered with tall trees.

"Look, there's a little pond in the middle of the island," Sara exclaimed.

"And a pretty little inlet at this end of it," Mrs. Harmon observed. "I suppose that's where the French ladies landed when they picnicked on the island."

Sara drew her brows together as she tried to imagine the French ladies in their long, billowing skirts, sitting on logs or rocks and eating their lunches on the wooded island across the way.

It seemed as if her father had read her thoughts, for he smiled at her and explained, "The French ladies who lived in Azilum became housekeepers and worked as hard in this wilderness as any pioneer woman. But even so, they brought with them their natural gaiety and tried to have as much pleasure in their surroundings as possible. So it is not hard to imagine that they would enjoy picnicking on this beautiful island."

As they looked at the peaceful scene, the curving river with its long island and the overhanging mountain on the far shore, Blair commented, "I can see why this would be a perfect hideaway for political exiles."

"Yes, it was very peaceful here after the horrors of the Reign of Terror in Paris," his father replied as they walked up the slope to the pavilion. "In 1794 the upper branches of the Susquehanna were sparsely populated, and it took days to reach Azilum by land and water from Philadelphia. The French émigrés felt quite safe here."

By the time they reached the picnic tables, they discovered that most of the visitors had left Azilum and they had the pavilion to themselves. Everyone was ravenous and it didn't take long for the cold beef sandwiches to disappear.

When they finished eating, the young people strolled down toward the river again.

"I want to show you something," Blair said. He pointed to a cut in Rummerfield Mountain across the way. "See those two stone turrets?"

Sara nodded, squinting at the two small round towers that stood out boldly on the edge of the mountain. "They look as if a castle was built up there on the mountain," she said curiously. "What are they?"

"They're the lookouts at the Marie Antoinette," Blair explained. "From there you can get a good panoramic view of Azilum. That's why the place is called the Marie Antoinette Lookout."

Sara caught her breath as she stared at the turrets. "You mean that's the Lookout where Mr. Cheney is staying?"

Blair nodded. "You can see the restaurant and gift shop from here, too."

The twins stared at the buildings with mounting interest. They were barely visible in a cut in the mountain where the highway circled upward along the river bluff. "You can even see one or two of the guest cottages," Blair added.

"I wonder which one Mr. Cheney is staying in," Sara mused.

At the mention of Mr. Cheney, Sam drew his brows together in a frown. "That guy bugs me. He sure is a mysterious character, eavesdropping on us in the garden and wanting to buy Princess Morning Star's pendant when it wasn't for sale. I wonder why he's so interested in the fleur-de-lis pendants?"

Sara shook her head. "Maybe if we could have heard more of the conversation he and his friend were having at the Prayer Rocks, we could have found out."

"Looks like you two super sleuths have more than one mystery to solve," grinned Blair.

"You're in on this with us," Sam reminded him, grinning back.

Just then they heard Mr. LaRue calling, "Blair, we're starting for home."

It was dark by the time they reached Wyalusing. A lamp glowed from the parlor where Abby McGuire was reading the Sunday paper. When the housekeeper heard them coming, she went out to the side porch to meet them.

"You had a phone call, Blair," she said as she took the empty picnic basket from him.

67

"Who was it?" Blair asked.

"I don't know," the housekeeper replied. "All he said was that his name was Jim Little Hawk and that he'd like to see you young folks tomorrow at the council grounds."

She was about to turn toward the kitchen but paused instead as if remembering something else. The twins and Blair exchanged curious looks when she added, "Oh, yes. He did mention that something important has turned up."

7

At the Lookout

"I WONDER what Jim wants to see us about," Blair said as they entered the council grounds the next morning.

They found the young guide leading a group of Cub Scouts across the grounds to the craft cabins. While the Scouts watched the exhibits and bought souvenirs, Jim hurried over to his friends.

"Hi, I'm glad you could come today," he said.

Without hesitation Blair asked, "What's up, Jim?"

"Has Princess Morning Star found her fleur-de-lis pendant?" Sara asked hopefully.

Jim shook his head. "No, and she's looked everywhere. I know because I helped her. We searched the trailer and the craft cabin but couldn't find it. She just hopes she hasn't lost it somewhere on the grounds."

"But she was sure she had it on when she changed from her ceremonial dress to her slacks and sweater," Sara remembered with a puzzled frown, "so it must be somewhere in the trailer."

"I know," Jim said with a bewildered shake of his head. "She thought so, too—but she just can't find it."

"Then what's turned up that you want to see us about?" Sam asked impatiently.

Jim flashed a guarded look around the council grounds, then lowered his voice. "I found out who that man was at the Prayer Rocks. The guy Mr. Cheney was talking to."

"Who is he?" Sara exclaimed. All three stood anxiously, waiting for him to continue.

"Well, Sam was right," Jim went on. "He's here for the Grand Council meeting, but he doesn't seem to be at all interested in any of the council proceedings. I heard Dad say that he's sort of a drifter, going here and there to places where Indian councils meet and setting up stands of cheap souvenirs to make a quick buck. He goes by the name of Orme and keeps to himself in that trailer of his back by Spirit Lake."

"So that's who that trailer belongs to," Sam exclaimed.

"He sure must want to keep to himself to be that far away from all the other council members," Sara mused. "It must be spooky staying back there alone."

Blair's mouth twitched playfully. "Yeah, and there's a full moon this week. Isn't that when the spirit of the old medicine man is supposed to be seen rising out of the waters of Spirit Lake, Jim?"

The Indian boy shifted uneasily from one foot to the other. Then he scoffed, "Aw, we don't believe in that old legend anymore."

Sam brought the subject around once more to Orme. "Now that we know who he is, what connection has he with Mr. Cheney?"

Jim opened his arms and let them flop. "That I don't know."

Sara let out a sigh. "If only we could have found out more of what they were talking about at the Prayer Rocks!"

"Whatever it was," Blair speculated, "it must have been something they didn't want anyone to hear. That's why they came down to the Rocks to talk."

"Well," Sam reflected, "since they're acting so mysterious, I think we better keep an eye on them."

The other three nodded their agreement.

"Oh-oh, here comes one of the Cub Scouts, and it looks as if he has a problem," Jim said.

"Probably doesn't have enough money to buy everything he sees," Sara said with a giggle.

Jim grinned ruefully. "That's usually the problem."

Blair glanced down at his watch. "We better get going, too. Dad wants me to help him get some lumber ready for delivery today. Want to come along and help, Sam?"

"Sure thing," Sam replied with interest. "I've never been around a lumberyard before."

They left Jim Little Hawk with his Cub Scouts and drove back to Wyalusing. On the way to the lumber company the boys dropped Sara off in front of the LaRue driveway.

A little miffed, she got out and frowned after the departing pickup. At least they could have asked her to go with them, she thought. It was queer how boys took girls for granted, as if they thought all girls had the same likes and dislikes. After all, Sara told herself with a pout, she could be as interested in a lumberyard as Sam.

The old Victorian house seemed especially quiet that

morning. Dad was off doing his research. Mr. LaRue was at the lumberyard, and she remembered that Abby McGuire was gone, too. Monday was her day off.

At least Mom was here, she discovered with relief as she climbed the porch steps and found her mother sitting in one of the wicker chairs, reading.

Sara sank into the chair next to her and wondered what she could do for the rest of the day.

Mrs. Harmon put her book aside and noticed the forlorn look on her daughter's face. "Were you deserted, too?" she asked.

Sara nodded glumly.

"Well, since we are alone today," her mother suggested, "how about going somewhere for lunch and doing a little exploring on our own?"

Sara brightened. "That'd be neat, Mom. Where to?"

"Well. . . ." Mrs. Harmon looked blank. "I don't know. We could get in the car and drive around, I suppose."

"But didn't Dad take the station wagon?"

Mrs. Harmon nodded. "But Charles said I could use his car if I wanted to go anywhere."

"Well, then let's go!" Sara said enthusiastically. As she jumped out of her chair, an idea popped into her head. "I know where we can go for lunch, Mom. To the Marie Antoinette Lookout."

"Where's that?" her mother asked.

"Up the highway on Route 6," Sara answered. "Yesterday at Azilum, Blair pointed it out to us. He said there is a restaurant there and a gift shop. And you can get a neat panoramic view of French Azilum from the turrets. That's why it's called the Marie Antoinette Lookout."

"Sounds good to me," Mom said, getting up and stretching. "Shall we leave now?"

Sara opened the door to the house. "I'll be ready as soon as I get my bag."

She ran up the stairs to her room, her heart beating fast. The Marie Antoinette Lookout was where Mr. Cheney was staying. Maybe she could find out something about him there. The idea excited her as she searched for her shoulder bag.

At last she found it, and flinging the strap over her shoulder, she hurried downstairs. A few minutes later Mrs. Harmon was backing Mr. LaRue's car out of the garage and they were on their way.

They drove up the highway past the Prayer Rocks. Soon they began climbing the side of Rummerfield Mountain. As they reached the crest and were rounding the downward sweep of a curve, Sara sighted a sign announcing the Marie Antoinette Inn.

"There it is!" she exclaimed, pointing out the wooden sign to her mother.

Beyond the sign was the restaurant, a homey-looking building with brown clapboard shingles, a green roof, and green shutters. Nearby was the gift shop, a miniature replica of the restaurant. Across from the restaurant and gift shop, along the edge of the mountain, was the Lookout with its two stone turrets.

Mrs. Harmon parked in front of one of the turrets where a blue and gold Pennsylvania Historical and Museum Commission marker explained the panorama across the river. She switched off the ignition key of the car and they sat a moment, reading the marker.

Azilum

The broad plain which can be seen from this point was the site, 1793-1803, of the French refugee colony. The Great House, built for Marie Antoinette and her son, was there and an entire village founded.

"Let's go into the turret and see the view," Mrs. Harmon suggested. "It will be interesting to see Azilum from this mountaintop. It will give us a different perspective."

Sara agreed and they got out of the car and walked over to the stone turret. In the shade of its green peaked roof, it was breezy and cool. Sara looked around at the vine-covered walls and flagstone floor. There was even a circular stone bench to sit on.

"It's like being inside the tower of a castle," she said, enchanted.

"It is lovely to sit here and see such a magnificent view," her mother agreed.

Sara looked out one of the arched stone windows to the horseshoe-curved river below and across to the crescent-shaped plain. Where once the French settlement had been was now peaceful countryside, with large dairy barns and square green and gold fields. At the northern end of the crescent plain the white LaPorte house sparkled in the sun, and near it they could see the tan roof of the pavilion where they had eaten their picnic supper yesterday. Directly in front of the pavilion, dividing the river into two channels, was the long wooded island, the favorite picnic spot of the French ladies. You could even see the little pond and the inlet from here.

Mom drew in a long satisfying breath. "What a magnificent panorama! The next time I come here, I'm going to bring a canvas and paint. Can you imagine what the river, the crescent plain, and the misty blue mountains in the distance would look like at sunset?"

"Beautiful!" Sara said. "But right now, Mom, I'm starved. What about lunch?"

74

Mrs. Harmon laughed. "So am I, honey. Let's go and see what's cookin'."

As they crossed the Lookout, Sara got her first glimpse of the six guest cottages nestled together on a grassy terrace to the left of the restaurant. Which one was Mr. Cheney staying in? she wondered. She'd have to find out.

They chose a small table by the window and ordered club sandwiches and iced tea. Sara fidgeted in her chair, wondering how she could find out about Mr. Cheney without Mom knowing and asking a million questions.

When her mother excused herself to go to the rest room, Sara saw her chance. Slipping out of her chair, she made her way to the counter where a waitress was adding up a check.

Realizing that the waitress was in a hurry, Sara asked quickly, "Do you know a Mr. Cheney?"

Without looking up, the busy waitress nodded. "Sure. He comes in here every night for dinner."

"Do you know what cottage he's staying in?" Sara ventured further.

"Number 4," the waitress answered briefly, ringing up the amount on the check and hurrying off with the change. Sara returned to their table just as Mom was coming out of the rest room.

They enjoyed the view of the mountains from the window while they ate their lunch. The club sandwiches and potato chips were delicious but filling, and Sara declared she didn't have room for dessert. Besides, she told herself, she couldn't wait a minute longer to find cabin number 4 and see if she could discover anything about the mysterious Mr. Cheney.

After they paid their bill and left the restaurant, Sara said casually, "Mom, while you're shopping, I'd like to wander around out here some more."

Her mother smiled. "All right. Meet me at the gift shop."

As she watched her mother enter the small shop next to the restaurant, Sara glanced at the line of parked cars by the Lookout. She was relieved that there was no gray van among them. If Mr. Cheney was not around, it would make her sleuthing that much easier.

She turned and hurried up the flagstone steps which led to the grassy terrace. She noticed that all the cottages were numbered and were exactly alike with small white porches and side steps leading up to them. No one seemed to be around at that moment, for which Sara was thankful.

She paused in front of cottage number 4 and stared up at it. She wished she could look inside, but the drapes were drawn together at the front window. Then she noticed that there were side windows in all the cottages.

She knew she shouldn't be peering into other people's windows, but since she was too curious to argue with her conscience, Sara slipped around to the side of Mr. Cheney's cottage. She didn't know what she was looking for or what she'd find. But who knows, she told herself, there may be something in that cottage that would give her a clue as to who Mr. Cheney was and why he was so interested in the fleur-de-lis pendants.

However, disappointment flooded through her when she discovered that the drapes were drawn across the side window, too. She was about to give up and join her mother at the gift shop when she heard a rustle in the long grass between the two cottages. Something was behind her. She could feel its presence.

Her heart beating wildly, she swung around, then leaned with relief against the side of the cottage when she spied the wagging tail and a pair of curious brown eyes looking up at her. She let out a tremulous giggle at the small brown-and-white-spotted dog.

"Hello there, fella," she said in a soft voice. "Where did you come from?"

The friendly little dog leaped up with his forepaws against her knees.

"Now don't bark and give us away," she whispered conspiratorially, reaching down to pat his wriggling body.

While she was bent over the dog, she spotted something white in the tall grass directly under the draped window. She reached through the grass and picked up a small, white card. She frowned down at it. It was a business card, and printed on it in black scrolls was the name *Hugh Cheney*.

Sara heard a threatening voice behind her. She forced herself to turn around, her heartbeat thumping in her throat.

Underneath the name were the words *Antique Jewelry* and a New York City address.

Sara drew in her breath. So that's who Mr. Cheney is, she thought. A buyer and seller of antique jewelry. No wonder he was interested in the fleur-de-lis pendants.

For a long moment Sara stood staring at the card, then she quickly slipped it into her shoulder bag and was about to leave when she heard a rustling in the grass again.

She thought the little dog was still there and was about to turn around when a low voice behind her said, "Are you looking for somebody, miss?"

Sara let out a small gasp. She knew that voice. She had heard it before.

In a threatening tone, the voice continued, "You shouldn't be so curious. It might lead to trouble."

Sara forced herself to turn around, her heartbeat thumping in her throat. But nobody was there now. Only a flash of a disappearing figure and the faint swish of grass told her that someone who didn't want to be seen had left suddenly.

8

The Ghost at Spirit Lake

SARA whirled and fled in the opposite direction, around the back of the cottages and down the flagstone steps. She didn't stop running until she reached the first stone turret. She slipped inside. She sank down on the circular bench, hidden from view in the cool shade.

While she waited for her heart to stop pounding, she thought about the voice she had heard. She was sure it was the same voice she had heard at the craft cabin and the Prayer Rocks—the voice that belonged to Mr. Cheney. And now he had seen her spying on his cottage. She gave a little shudder as she remembered his threatening tone, warning her not to be so curious—that it might lead to trouble.

After several long moments, and still a bit shaken, she left the turret to join her mother at the gift shop. As she was crossing the Lookout, she glanced again at the parked cars, and this time she noticed a gray van parked at the far end. Mr. Cheney must have returned while she was exploring his cottage. Perfect timing, she thought grimly.

When she arrived at the gift shop, she discovered that her mother had already selected several small items. Sara was glad that Mom was busy at the cash register and didn't notice her flushed face or how excited she still was. Taking a deep breath to calm herself, she waited patiently until the purchases were paid for, then followed her mother out of the gift shop to Mr. LaRue's car.

When they arrived back at Wyalusing, they learned that the boys had just returned from the lumberyard. While Mom went upstairs to put away her purchases, Sara and the boys went into the kitchen for something cool to drink. While they were sitting around the kitchen table, Sara told about her adventure at the Marie Antoinette Lookout.

"It's too bad you didn't get a look inside that cottage," Sam said. "You might have found out something about Mr. Cheney."

"Maybe it was just as well she couldn't if Mr. Cheney was there," Blair reasoned. "If he warned Sara not to be so curious, he must have been upset to find her snooping around, and if he had found her looking inside his cottage, he might have really flipped."

"Yeah, I guess you're right," Sam said, looking with brotherly concern at his twin.

"I did find this in the grass just outside his window," Sara said as she opened her shoulder bag and took out Mr. Cheney's business card. "It must have blown out of his window when it was open."

Sam's eyebrows shot up as he read the card. "A dealer in

antique jewelry!" he exclaimed. "Hey, things are beginning to look up. Now we know why Mr. Cheney has a thing about the fleur-de-lis pendants. He probably recognized them as very old and valuable and wanted to buy them."

"Then why didn't he come right out and ask Blair's father if he would sell his pendant?" Sara wondered.

"Maybe that's what he was going to do, but decided to do a little eavesdropping first to find out how much the pendant was worth," Sam replied.

"Well, he sure got an earful if he heard Dad telling about the trust fund Claude set up for Jacques' heirs," Blair said anxiously. "He'd know that trust fund would be worth plenty today."

Sam pursed his lips. "What gets me, Blair, is how he knew your dad had the fleur-de-lis pendant in the first place."

"I think the card Sara found answers that," Blair replied. "You see, Dad had inquired at several antique jewelry firms in New York and Philadelphia about Jacques' pendant. He thought maybe if some of the dealers had seen it, they could give him a clue to the whereabouts of Jacques' descendants. If Mr. Cheney is a dealer himself, he probably found out about it from the other dealers."

"Sounds logical," agreed Sam.

Just then the phone in the kitchen rang and Blair jumped up to answer it.

"Sure—sure," he said with a smile on his round face. "Hey, that'd be neat. Thanks. See you there."

When he returned to the table, he said, "That was Jim Little Hawk. He called to invite us to the tribal dances at the council grounds tonight."

"Sounds great," the twins chorused.

"What time?" asked Sara.

"He said after it gets dark. They're going to have the

dances around a big bonfire."

Sara picked up her can of cola but stopped with it in midair. "They are?"

"Sure," replied Blair. "Jim said the dances are more effective by firelight."

Sam grinned over at his sister. "Don't worry, Twinny. There's a full moon tonight. That should brighten things up for us."

The beat of a tom tom greeted them as they walked up the road to the council grounds that night. Sara felt a tremor of excitement at the sound of the haunting rhythm.

They joined the outer circle of spectators that stood around a huge bonfire in the open space in back of the longhouse. In the inner circle of dancers, a drummer was beating out the rhythm of the dance on a hollowed-out log, covered with a thin deerskin. Two other men were vigorously shaking turtle-shell rattles.

Jim Little Hawk made his way through the spectators to where they were standing. "You're just in time for the first dance," he told them.

At that moment the drumbeats throbbed louder and faster, calling the dancers to form a circle around the fire. When the circle was formed, the beats softened with the pulse of the turtle rattles and the wistful, haunting chants of the women in accompaniment.

The men led off in the circle, counterclockwise, with the women closing in behind, the fringes on their deerskin gowns swaying gracefully to the rhythm of their feet. They moved one foot lightly forward and then backward, their bodies straight and their arms hung relaxed and still. Their steps were so graceful that their moccasined feet seemed to be gliding on air.

82

At the sudden crescendo of the drums, the dancers quickened their steps. Their agility and lightness of foot amazed the twins. As Sara glanced at the swaying forms, silhouetted against the fire, she felt as if she were back in time, when this same dance was performed on this mountaintop centuries ago. As Jim had said, the dances by firelight were certainly effective.

Abruptly the drumbeats stopped and the dance ended. The performers left the circle to rest a moment during which the drummer continued to chant until another dance was formed.

"The next dance is the peace pipe dance," Jim explained as the dancers joined hands this time in the ring around the fire. During one part of the dance in ancient calumet, or peace pipe, was passed around the circle of dancers. Then the leader dropped the hand of one of his partners and drew the dancers into a tight circle around him.

"The circle of friendship," Jim said, his dark eyes sparkling in the firelight. "And now the chain of friendship."

No sooner had he explained than the dancers left the circle and joined hands with the spectators until a long chain of dancers and spectators was formed.

Sara glanced over at her brother whose hand was grasped by Princess Morning Star. Sam was grinning and didn't seem to mind being part of the dance. Sara was thrilled that her hand was held in a firm grip of friendship by a smiling young Indian boy.

After the peace pipe dance, the drum and chanting stopped and the dancers mingled with the spectators. Sam sought out Sara and gave her a nudge as he cocked his head in the direction of a group of men.

"There's Orme," he said in a low voice.

Sara glanced quickly in the direction Sam had indicated.

The stocky Indian was laughing at something one of the men was saying.

"For someone who's unsociable, he seems to be having a good time," Sara remarked.

"Who wouldn't on a night like this," Sam replied. "I'd say all the council members are here for the dances."

When Jim and Blair found them, Jim said, "This is intermission. Let's take a walk. It's getting hot here by the fire with so many people around."

"Good idea," Blair agreed. "Let's walk back by Spirit Lake. I'd like to see it in the moonlight."

Sam looked at Sara with a teasing expression. "Yeah, maybe we'll see the spirit of that ancient medicine man rise out of the water."

"You both think I'm chicken," Sara said with a toss of her head. "Okay, let's go!"

Jim led the way down the path through the cool, dark woods to the pond. The full moon was caught in the branches of a tall oak and a thin mist hung low over the black waters of Spirit Lake.

Although she tried not to show her uneasiness to the others, Sara felt a little shiver creep down her back. She jumped when Jim, looking around the pond bank, suddenly drew in a quick breath.

"See a ghost?" Blair called out in a laughing voice.

"I see something," Jim answered. "There's a light through those trees across the pond."

Their heads swiveled in the direction he was pointing.

"That's where Orme's trailer is," Sam said in a low voice. "Maybe he left a light on when he left it tonight."

"Let's find out," Blair suggested and was off before any of them could stop him.

They followed, making their way along the shadowy edge

of the pond until they came to the small clearing where Orme's pickup and trailer were parked. As they peered out from behind the trees, Sara let out a low gasp. "Look! Someone's in the trailer."

Curiously they watched a dark silhouette moving about inside the trailer. As they edged closer to get a better look, Sam inadvertently stepped on a fallen branch and it snapped loudly in two. They drew back, their hearts throbbing, as the light went out and the trailer stood in quiet darkness.

Sara thought she heard the faint squeaking of a door opening and then closing. But she couldn't be sure. It was dark in the clearing, shadowed by overhanging trees. A frightening thought flashed through her mind. Whoever they had seen inside the trailer might now be outside.

"Let's go back to the log bench," she called out in a hushed, frightened voice.

Sara gave a choked cry. "Let's get out of here!" Jim leaped off the bench and the others followed.

85

The boys didn't object, and with Jim in the lead they retraced their steps along the pond bank. When they were seated on the bench, Jim said curiously, "I wonder who was in Orme's trailer."

"It couldn't have been Orme," Sam said. "Sara and I saw him at the dances."

"And he was still talking to those men when we left the bonfire," added Sara.

"It sure was weird that that light flicked off as soon as we got to the trailer," Blair mused.

"Whoever was in there must have heard us," Sam said. "Me and my clumsy feet!"

They fell silent as they waited for the sound of the drum to call them back to the dance. Sara kept wondering who the shadowy figure was that they had seen in Orme's trailer. What was he doing there, and why had he quickly turned off the light when he had heard them?

These thoughts spun around in her head as she watched the moon, a pale wavery orb, reflect through the mist on the dark mirror of the pond. On the far bank the deep hemlocks brightened in its glow like an eerie backdrop to a stage setting. Suddenly, in the pale, silvery light appeared a ghostly form that seemed to be rising out of the mist of Spirit Lake.

Sara blinked her eyes several times to see if she were just imagining the thing that she saw. But when she sensed Sam's body stiffen next to hers, she knew she wasn't imagining—that the ghostly figure was real.

Blair and Jim saw it, too. They could scarcely believe their eyes as they stared at the horrible black face that shone through the mist at them. The moon spotlighted it so that they could see plainly the round white eyes, beaked nose, large thick red lips, and long strands of black and white hair that hung down limply on either side of its huge head.

The four young people sat frozen. It was not until the first moment of shock had passed that they stared at one another incredulously.

"It-it's the spirit of the ancient medicine man!" Jim quavered through tight lips.

Sara gave a choked cry. "Let's get out of here!"

Jim leaped off the bench and the others followed as he sprinted down the path leading to the council grounds.

9
Caught in the Act

SARA glanced over her shoulder to see if the ghost was following them. In her vivid imagination she could picture that horrible black face drifting through the mist on the pond and among the dark trees. But in reality the spirit had disappeared as suddenly as it had appeared, and the misty pond lay undisturbed and peaceful once more.

As they neared the council grounds, the sound of drumbeats started up, but they were all too shaken at what they had seen at Spirit Lake to stop to watch the next dance. Instead, Jim waved them on to his trailer, and Blair and the twins followed. When he swung open the door, they piled in after him and sank down on the carpeted floor.

Jim caught his breath and said, "I need something cold to

drink. Mom made lemonade. Anyone want some?"

"I sure could use a glass," Sara gasped.

"That goes for me, too," said Sam.

Jim went to a small refrigerator and brought out a frosty pitcher. With trembling hands he poured the contents into plastic glasses. As they sipped their cold drinks, Blair kept shaking his head and mumbling, "I don't believe it! I just don't believe it! It *couldn't* have been a ghost."

Jim regarded him curiously. "Well, then, what did we see? It had to be something."

"Yes, all four of us saw it," Sara confirmed in a quavering voice.

Sam sat hunched over, the faraway look on his face that was always there when he was thinking of something. Finally he looked up at Jim and asked, "Does Orme leave his trailer any time during the day?"

Jim was puzzled at Sam's question but nodded. "Sure. Orme has a souvenir stand on the council grounds. Sometimes he gets a boy to watch it, but he's there, himself, most of the time."

"What are you getting at, Sam?" asked Sara.

"Well, I was thinking that we could meet here again tomorrow, and while Orme is at his stand, we can look around his trailer. Maybe we can find a clue to discover who was there tonight."

"What does that have to do with the ghost?" Blair protested.

"I don't know," Sam admitted, "but I'd sure like to find out who was inside Orme's trailer tonight and why he turned off the light when he heard us outside."

"Whoever it was didn't want to be seen," Blair said flatly.

"But why?" Sara wondered with a puzzled shake of her head.

"You know, I think Sam has a good idea," Jim spoke up. "Let's meet here early tomorrow and have a look around Orme's trailer."

They finished their drinks and put the empty glasses in the sink. Before they said good night to Jim, the Indian boy warned, "Let's keep this to ourselves for the time being. If word got around about what we saw tonight, everyone at the Grand Council would be upset, and my dad might not like the idea of our nosing around Spirit Lake again."

"Right," Blair agreed, giving Sara and Sam a meaningful look. "We won't even tell our parents."

As they drove back to Wyalusing, Sara kept seeing, in her mind's eye, the ugly black face peering at them through the misty darkness. There was something weird about that face.

"It certainly didn't look human," she spoke her thoughts aloud. "It almost seemed as if it could have been the spirit of that ancient medicine man rising out of Spirit Lake."

Neither one of the boys teased her about the ghost this time. Sam just took a deep breath and said, "There must be some logical explanation for what we saw tonight."

"Yeah, but what?" Blair mumbled.

Sam had no answer for that and they rode the rest of the way home in silence.

Later that night dark clouds scudded across the face of the moon and thunder rumbled over Rummerfield Mountain. As the storm drew near, Sara tossed restlessly in her bed. She dreamed that a black, ugly head was chasing her around Mr. LaRue's garden, its white eyes blazing in the dark and an evil, rumbling sound coming from its thick red lips. It was coming closer and closer. When a clawlike hand reached out to grab her, she screamed and sat up in bed with a start.

"Hey, hey, take it easy," her father spoke softly, his hand on her shoulder. "You must have had quite a dream."

Sara sank back against her pillows, weak with relief that it had been only a dream. "I did," she murmured in a shaky voice.

"Probably the storm brought it on," Dad said, turning toward the French door when a flash of lightning brightened the room, followed by a loud rumble of thunder.

Sara wanted to tell her father about the real cause of her dream, but she had promised the boys she wouldn't breathe a word.

She nestled down under the covers again. "Thanks, Dad. I'm okay now," she said in a small voice. "The storm's moving on."

He got up to leave but kept the door to the adjoining room open. Amid the fading rumbles of thunder, Sara dropped off to sleep again and slept soundly for the rest of the night.

Blair had to deliver some lumber for his father the next morning, but before he went to the lumberyard, he drove the twins to the council grounds. "Tell Jim I'll be back in about an hour," he called to them as he drove off.

Jim met them at the totem and when they explained that Blair would be here later, he replied, "That's okay. Orme hasn't opened his stand yet."

While they waited for Orme to leave his trailer, they sauntered idly around the council grounds. Some early tourists had arrived, and the council members were busy opening their craft cabins and stands to get ready for the day.

"Don't you have to guide this morning?" Sara asked.

Jim shook his head. "We take turns and another guy offered to take my place today."

They paused in front of the longhouse and Sam glanced curiously at the bark building. "You know, Jim," he said, "you never showed us inside this place. How about a tour while we wait for Orme?"

"Okay, come on," Jim said.

He pulled back the bearskin that hung over the entrance, and they followed him into the dim, rectangular building. He pointed to the stone fire pit in the middle of the ground floor where the chiefs and head women met in council.

"They usually hold council meetings in the afternoon," Jim explained. "Nobody is allowed inside here then, so this is a good time to show you around."

From the roof poles hung tanned animal skins and feathers, just as they had hung on similar roof poles centuries ago. "Three or more families used to live together in the longhouse, and from the things that hung on the roof poles, you could tell which section of the longhouse belonged to which family," Jim said.

While Jim was explaining, Sara walked around and gazed at the pretty shawls and colorfully beaded clothing that hung on wooden pegs along the walls. She recognized some of them as the ceremonial costumes the dancers had worn the previous night. Above the costumes she spied a row of carved masks, grimacing down at her. She didn't remember seeing a dance where the masks were worn, but they may have missed that one.

Sara moved closer to the masks so that she could see them better. They resembled large false faces. Some were made of wood and some of corn husks. Her curious gaze ran from face to face.

Suddenly she gave a start as her eyes fixed upon a grotesque black mask. It had a beaked nose, round white eyes, thick red lips, and long strands of black and white hair that hung limply on either side.

She drew in her breath then let out a shrill cry of surprise.

92

"It-it's the ghost!" she shrilled. "The ghost at Spirit Lake!"

The boys walked over and looked at the mask she was pointing to.

"Oh, wow!" cried Sam. "It sure is."

Astonished, Jim stared at the ugly mask. "Why, it's the mask the dancer impersonating the medicine man wears in the False Face Dance!" he exclaimed. "I hadn't thought about it before, but it does look like the ghost we saw last night."

"But why would a medicine man wear such a gruesome mask?" Sara asked with a shiver.

"Because in the old days the medicine mask was worn to chase off evil spirits," Jim told her, "so it had to be ugly and threatening."

Sara and Sam exchanged glances. "Then the ghost we saw last night wasn't a ghost at all but someone wearing this mask," Sara reasoned.

"Someone impersonating the ghost of the dead medicine man," Sam added grimly.

"Yeah, that could be," Jim agreed, his eyebrows drawn into a frowning line.

Sara's shock turned to sudden anger. "What a weird thing for anybody to do—scaring us away from Spirit Lake with a medicine mask! Who would do such a thing?"

Sam's brooding eyes fastened on the black mask. "Maybe the person we saw in Orme's trailer last night. Maybe he didn't want us spying around and was the one who scared us off."

Quickly, Sara's mind flashed back to the night before. She remembered how, after the light in the trailer had been extinguished, she thought she had heard the faint squeaking of the door opening and then closing. She remembered the scary feeling she had that whoever had been inside the trailer had come outside. That was just before they had run back to the bench on the other side of the pond.

"Would whoever it was have had time to come here to the longhouse to get the mask and then be back at Spirit Lake by the time we saw it?" she wondered doubtfully.

"Sure," Jim spoke up. "It didn't take us long to run back here from Spirit Lake after we saw the ghost."

"Jim's right," Sam agreed. "It wouldn't take long, especially for someone who knows where the masks are kept."

"Then it must be someone belonging to the council," Sara said slowly. "But who? And why would anybody be snooping inside Orme's trailer and not wanting to be seen?"

"That, Twinny, is what we're going to try to find out today," Sam replied.

They took one more look at the ugly mask, then turned to the door flap and let themselves out of the longhouse. As they walked past the craft cabins, a familiar voice called out, "Hello, there. You're here early today."

Princess Morning Star was standing in the doorway of her cabin. She had on her ceremonial dress and was wearing colorful strands of beads around her neck. But the fleur-de-lis pendant was missing.

As they walked into the craft cabin, Sara said, "You haven't found your pendant, have you?"

Princess Morning Star's smile faded. "No, it is gone and I do not know if I shall ever find it." She shook her head, puzzled. "I am sure I had put it away carefully in my jewel chest with my ceremonial beads."

"Could it have been stolen?" Sam asked bluntly.

Princess Morning Star looked up with surprise. "Oh, I hardly think so. You see, we don't even lock our doors at the Grand Council. It is considered an insult to lock our trailers. We all trust one another. If one needs anything, one has

94

only to ask for it and it will be given. That is the Indian way."

"Then maybe one of the sightseers took it," Sam persisted.

Princess Morning Star shook her head doubtfully. "Unless they are invited, non-Indian visitors are kept away from our living quarters by guides like Jim." She fell silent for a moment, her face grim. "I just can't imagine anyone here at the Grand Council taking it. Everyone knows how much I value it. It is a family heirloom."

"I know," Sara murmured. "Mr. LaRue would like it found, too, so that he can find Jacques' descendant and fulfill Claude's wishes of bringing the LaRue family together again."

"Mr. LaRue is a kind and generous man," Princess Morning Star said with a sad little sigh. "I wish I could find the pendant, if only for him."

At that moment a woman hurried up to the craft cabin. "I'm going into town to do some shopping," she called to Princess Morning Star. "Do you want to come along?"

Princess Morning Star looked up and shook her head. "I can't leave the cabin right now."

"I'll be gone for only about a half hour," the woman persisted.

"I would like to go, but I have just set up my display and I have nobody to be here in my place."

Sara spoke up eagerly, "I'll watch your display, Princess Morning Star. I'd love to stay here until you get back."

Princess Morning Star hesitated. "Oh, but I don't like to impose."

"You wouldn't be," Sara assured her. "Honestly. It'll be fun to watch the display for you." She paused with a giggle. "Who knows, maybe I'll even make a sale."

"Well...." Princess Morning Star finally agreed, and after showing Sara the cash box and explaining the price of the turquoise jewelry, she hurried off with her friend.

Sara assumed the place of importance behind the display table. Grinning over at her brother and Jim, she quipped, "What can I do for you, sirs. A pretty turquoise ring, perhaps? Here's a nice gentleman's belt buckle for only...."

"Oh, come off it, Twinny," laughed Sam. "Come on, Jim. Let's get going. Isn't that Orme over there, opening up his stand?"

Jim glanced across the way at the big man assembling feathered headbands, toy tomahawks, and other trinkets on the counter of his stand. He nodded. "I guess it's safe to go back to his trailer now."

Before they left, Sam told Sara, "When Princess Morning Star gets back, meet us at Spirit Lake. Maybe Blair will be here by then."

"Will do," Sara said. She gave a little smile of satisfaction as she watched the boys make their way toward the back of the council grounds. She was glad that Princess Morning Star had entrusted her to watch the display. It would be much more fun trying to sell turquoise jewelry than to search the spooky woods around Orme's trailer.

Back in the woods Sam and Jim made their way to Spirit Lake. "First, let's search the place where we saw the ghost," Sam suggested. "Then we can look around the trailer."

Jim agreed and led the way around the pond to the thick stand of hemlocks where they had seen the ugly mask peering across the water at them. They searched the hemlocks thoroughly but found nothing except a broken branch.

They made their way to the trailer and searched the woods around it. They even walked along the narrow graveled road that led from the top of the bluff to the highway below. There were no fresh tire marks. Nothing.

Back in the clearing, Sam studied the trailer curiously. He wondered what it looked like inside. He walked up to the vehicle and peered through the window. Suddenly he let out a surprised cry and motioned quickly for Jim.

"Look in there," he said excitedly. "On the table."

Jim pressed his eye close to the window and sucked in his breath. There on a small foldaway table was the missing fleur-de-lis pendant.

"No wonder whoever was in the trailer last night didn't want us snooping around," Sam told him.

But Jim wasn't listening to Sam's reasoning. "Why the thieving. . . ." A surge of cold anger shook his voice. "I'm going in there right now and get it." And before Sam could stop him, Jim flung open the door of the trailer and disappeared inside.

At that same moment Sam's sharp ears heard the sound of twigs snapping under heavy feet. Through the trees he glimpsed two men coming around the pond bank.

"Hey, Jim! Get out!" he warned as loudly as he could.

When Jim didn't respond, Sam scrambled through the open trailer door. He closed it behind him, just as the two men came into view of the trailer.

Jim looked up from the foldaway table. At the expression on Sam's face, he asked, "What's the matter?"

"Orme's coming!" Sam gasped.

Jim drew in a quick breath. "But how can that be? We saw him opening up his stand."

"I know, but Mr. Cheney's with him and they're coming here."

Jim's gaze flew to the window. "Oh, wow, we're caught. We can't get out now. They're heading for the trailer."

97

"Get down!" Sam hissed. "Maybe they won't come in."

"What'll I do with this?" croaked Jim, taking the fleur-de-lis pendant from his pocket. "If they find us, they might search us—especially if they discover the pendant's missing."

Sam looked around the cluttered one room of the little trailer and gave a low moan. "Oh, man, there's nowhere to hide in here."

"Here they come," Jim wailed softly.

Sam grabbed the pendant and looked desperately around him. A large can of coffee stood open on top of the stove. Fortunately the can was almost full and Sam pushed the pendant deep down between the brown grains to the bottom. No sooner had he done this than the trailer door flew open and the two men entered.

Orme's huge bulk almost filled the room. He stood there, his mouth opened with surprise. His eyes widened in disbelief as he stared at the two frightened boys.

Recovering from his shock, his gaze flew to the little table. He lumbered up to it, speechless for a second, then he boomed, "The pendant! Where's the pendant? I had it right here on this table."

Mr. Cheney's shrewd eyes raked the boys with suspicion. "So that's what you two are doing here. Well, your little game of spying is over now, boys. Hand over the pendant."

Jim's body tensed. "It's not yours," he accused. "It belongs to Princess Morning Star and you stole it!"

Mr. Cheney's face was dark with anger. His eyes blazed. "If you won't hand over the pendant, we'll have to search you," he snapped. "Pull out your pockets and take off your shoes."

The silent boys obeyed, and after Orme had frisked them thoroughly, Mr. Cheney turned to his friend and said icily,

"You should have hidden the pendant better, Orme. Keeping it here on your table in view of everybody was stupid. Now our original plan is ruined and we'll have to sell it the best way we can."

"But nobody ever comes back to my trailer," argued the big man. "That's why I parked it way back here."

He swung around and while the boys put their shoes on, he started to search through the clutter, turning over cartons of souvenirs and pushing aside piles of clothing and newspapers. He opened cabinet doors then slammed them shut. He even looked in the oven and the tiny refrigerator.

"We can't hunt for it now with these two here," Mr. Cheney grumbled. "Someone from the council grounds might wander back here and see us holding them. You're stupid to think that nobody ever comes here. I've a mind to cut you out of this deal right now."

"You better not," Orme threatened, rolling his hands into two huge fists. He turned a dark glance at the boys. "Where did you two hide it?" he roared.

Mr. Cheney gave a bitter laugh. "They won't tell you, Orme, but we have ways to make them talk." His small dark eyes darted about the cluttered trailer. "Do you have any rope in all this litter?"

Sam tensed himself, ready to leap. When Orme turned away to get the rope, Sam gave Jim a slight nod and both boys made a break for the door.

"Oh, no you don't!" roared Orme, reaching out quickly and grabbing Jim by the collar. He held him like a cat holds a mouse.

Mr. Cheney grabbed Sam around the waist and a hard hand closed over his mouth so that the boys couldn't yell for help. Sam tried to fight back, kicking and struggling against the hold, but it did him little good. The more he struggled

99

the tighter Mr. Cheney held him, his grip like a steel vise.

Holding Jim with one powerful arm, Orme reached into a small cabinet under the sink and drew out a coil of clothesline. Grinning menacingly at the boys, he mumbled, "Always carry this with me. Comes in handy more ways than one."

"We'll tie them up and gag them," Mr. Cheney said, a cruel smile twisting his thin lips. Sam was shaking in his sneakers as the man began to pull the ropes tight around his wrists. Orme tackled Jim and while they worked, Mr. Cheney barked out his plan.

"We got to get them out of here so they can't squeal on us. I'll drive the van back here, and we'll take them to a

Orme plastered electrical tape across the boys' mouths so that they couldn't call for help.

place where nobody will find them. They'll stay there until we find the pendant or until they decide to tell us where they hid it."

"What place do you have in mind?" asked Orme.

"A place called Homet's Ferry," Mr. Cheney replied. "It's an old landing across the river. Heard some locals talking about it at the Lookout. They said nobody lives near the landing, and only a fisherman now and then goes over there to fish."

"Seems like a lot of effort just for one lousy gold pendant," grumbled Orme.

"Ho-ho!" laughed Mr. Cheney. "That antique pendant is worth more than you think."

Orme only grunted and Mr. Cheney left for the van. While he was gone, Orme found some electrical tape which he plastered across the boys' mouths so that they couldn't call for help.

As they waited for Mr. Cheney's return, Sam breathed a silent and desperate prayer, "*Please*, God, help us!"

In a short while they heard the crunch of tires on the gravel road. The boys were then led out to the gray van they had seen at the Prayer Rocks.

While the two men were busy unlocking the back of the van and getting Jim into it, Sam hurriedly carved the letters HF with the toe of his sneaker into the bare patch of ground by the trailer step. He had just enough time to make a squiggle that resembled an S underneath the letters before the two men turned and motioned him into the van.

He was pushed onto the floor next to Jim, with Orme crouched over them. Mr. Cheney got into the cab, and a moment later they were bumping down the gravel road that led to the highway.

10
Missing

SARA was wrapping a pretty turquoise necklace in some tissue paper when she glimpsed Blair striding past the cabin. "Excuse me," she said to the lady who was waiting for her purchase to be wrapped.

Sara stepped over to the door of the cabin and called to Blair. The boy turned, surprised to see her at the craft cabin. "What are you doing here?" he asked. "Where are Sam and Jim?"

"Wait a sec and I'll explain," Sara said, hurrying back to her customer. Blair waited by the door while she finished wrapping the necklace and took the money for it.

"That's the fourth piece of jewelry I sold," she said triumphantly when the lady had left the cabin. "I'm mind-ing the store while Princess Morning Star is in town shopping. Sam and Jim are at Spirit Lake."

"I'll go back there and meet them," Blair said. And before Sara could expand on her success as a salesclerk, he was off with a wave of his hand.

About ten minutes later, Princess Morning Star returned to the cabin. "I hope I haven't kept you here too long," she apologized, glancing down at her watch. "My goodness, it's been almost an hour."

"That's okay," Sara replied. "The time went fast and I sold four pieces of jewelry."

"Good for you!" Princess Morning Star praised. "How about treating you to some lunch in my trailer?"

"Thanks, I'd like that a lot," Sara said, "but I promised to meet the guys by Spirit Lake when you returned."

Just then another customer stepped into the cabin and Sara made her departure. "Any time you want me to help out again, I'd love to," she called over her shoulder to Princess Morning Star. "It was fun."

And it was fun, too, she thought as she made her way across the council grounds. While she had been working at the craft cabin, selling jewelry for the Navajo reservation, she had felt she was a part of the Indian council and not just a sightseer. You get a lot more out of something if you help out with it than if you just stand back and look on, she decided.

When she reached Spirit Lake, she found Blair sitting alone on the log bench. When he saw her coming, he looked up with a puzzled expression on his face.

"What's the matter?" she called out. "Where are Sam and Jim?"

"That's just it," Blair answered. "I've looked all over and can't find them."

103

Sara glanced at the pond. It was serene and empty this morning, not a ripple disturbing its dark surface. She looked back through the trees in the direction of the trailer. "Did you look around Orme's trailer?"

Blair nodded. "I even peeked through the windows, and I called and called. I just can't find them." He took a deep breath. "Let's go back to the council grounds and ask around. Maybe they're there for some reason."

"I didn't see them while I was at the craft cabin," Sara said doubtfully.

"Well, maybe they got tired of looking around here and went to Jim's trailer," Blair said. "Let's look there first."

They retraced their steps to the council grounds. When they came to Jim's trailer, one of the guides hurried up to them. Smiling apologetically, he said, "I'm sorry but no one is permitted here except the council members."

"Oh, we forgot," Sara said.

Blair explained, "We're Jim Little Hawk's friends and we're looking for him."

"Then let's see if he's here," invited the guide.

He knocked on the door of the trailer and they called Jim's name, but no one answered.

"Why don't you ask around at the craft cabins," the guide suggested. "The people there would know if Jim is on the grounds."

"Good idea," Blair said. After they thanked the guide, they made their way across the council grounds.

But at every craft cabin the answer was the same. No one had seen Jim or Sam.

"They don't seem to be anywhere around," Blair said finally. "It's as if they had just disappeared into space."

At Blair's words a tingling chill passed through Sara and something inside her set up a warning. People don't just disappear into space—they either leave on their own accord or are forced to leave. And if Sam and Jim had left Spirit Lake on their own, Sam would have let her know. She was sure of it. If he couldn't come himself to let her know, he would have left a message.

"That's it!" Sara exclaimed. "Sam must have left a message that we overlooked. Let's go back to Spirit Lake and hunt for it."

"Okay, but I'm hungry," Blair remarked. "Tell you what, let's get a couple of burgers and some Cokes at the refreshment stand and take them with us."

"Good idea," Sara agreed.

They carried their lunch back to Spirit Lake, and while they sat on the log bench by the pond, Sara told Blair about the medicine mask they had seen in the longhouse.

"So that's what that ugly face was all about," Blair exclaimed. "But who was wearing the mask? Why would anyone want to frighten us away from Spirit Lake?"

"Sam thinks it has something to do with that prowler in Orme's trailer last night," Sara replied.

When they finished their lunch, they searched around the pond bank and back at Orme's trailer for a message Sam may have left. But they found nothing.

Sara slumped down on the little iron step leading up to the trailer door and cupped her chin in the palm of her hand. What had become of her brother and Jim, she wondered. She tried to recall everything Sam had told her that morning. Before he and Jim had left her at the craft cabin, Sam had definitely told her to meet them at Spirit Lake. After telling her that, it was not like Sam to leave for any reason without letting her know.

A little chill of anxiety came over her. It was that sixth sense that the twins often had when they knew that one of them was in trouble. And Sara had that feeling right now.

She tried to be rational to think things out. If Sam went somewhere else and couldn't tell her, he would have certainly left a message of some kind. That she was sure of. But where was it? They had looked around Orme's trailer and had found nothing. There was no message secured to a tree trunk or to the log bench—the obvious places to leave a note.

With a long sigh Sara glanced down at her feet. There was only one thing now that she could do, and she knew it was the only thing that would help. She closed her eyes and said a little silent prayer. "O God, help us find Sam and Jim, and if they're in trouble, please keep them safe."

She opened her eyes and idly looked down at the small grassless patch of ground by the step where she sat. Suddenly she blinked her eyes, and leaning over, she examined the patch curiously. It was then that she spied something carved roughly on the bare ground.

She scrambled off the step and studied the wavy lines. They were difficult to make out, but as she stared at them, the letters HF formed in front of her. Her heart did a flip-flop when she spied the squiggle in the ground below the letters.

"Found anything?" Blair asked as he squatted down beside her.

"Somebody recently carved the letters HF on the ground here," she said breathlessly.

Blair stared at the crooked lines. "Hey, I believe you're right!" Looking closer, he exclaimed, "That squiggle underneath the letters looks like an S."

"I thought so, too," Sara said, growing more excited. "Sam did leave us a message, Blair. But what's he trying to tell us? What do the letters HF mean?"

"HF," Blair pondered, drawing his brows together. "Sounds like someone's initials."

"It's not anyone here that Sam and I know," Sara said slowly, "and yet HF must stand for *something* we know, Blair, or Sam wouldn't have carved those letters. Maybe they mean a place."

"Yeah, that must be it," Blair mused. He closed his eyes and tried to concentrate. "HF, HF," he said under his breath.

Abruptly he straightened up and his face brightened. "Of course! Homet's Ferry!"

Sara's expression was one of blank confusion. "But what could Sam mean by that?"

"Maybe he meant that's where he and Jim went," Blair said. He paused, frowning. "But why they'd want to go way over there is beyond me. And how could they get to Homet's Ferry in the first place without a car?"

"Unless someone drove them there," Sara half-whispered. "Maybe they were forced to go."

Blair's eyebrows shot up with surprise. "Forced to go! What do you mean by that?"

"I mean why would Sam leave us this obscure message unless he had to?" Sara replied. "If he and Jim had decided to go there on their own, he would have come back to Princess Morning Star's cabin and told me."

"Yeah, or you'd think they'd wait until I got back with the pickup." Blair ran his fingers through his dark hair. "But why would he and Jim be forced to go to Homet's Ferry? It doesn't make sense."

"Maybe someone didn't want them snooping around here," Sara said in a low tone. "You know what happened last night when we were snooping around—how someone scared us away with the medicine mask."

107

Blair nodded. "It's pretty obvious that someone doesn't want us around. But what has that got to do with Homet's Ferry?"

Sara shook her head. "I don't know, but I think it's time we ask Orme a few questions."

"So do I," Blair said grimly. "Come on, let's go."

But when they arrived back at the council grounds, they were surprised to find that Orme was not at his souvenir stand. The young boy who was watching it was waiting on a family with three small children, each one of them wanting a feathered headband. Sara and Blair waited impatiently until the sale was made, then they asked the boy if he knew where Orme was.

The boy glanced up after depositing the money in a cigar box. "He left with some guy quite a while ago," he answered vaguely. "Didn't say where he was going or when he'd be back."

"What did the guy that he left with look like?" asked Blair.

The boy cocked his head thoughtfully. "Well, he was tall and thin, I guess, and had a beard."

Sara threw Blair a quick look. "Mr. Cheney!"

As they left the souvenir stand, she asked desperately, "Would you drive over to Homet's Ferry, Blair? I don't know why, but that's probably where we'll find Sam and Jim." With a thin edge of fright in her voice, she added, "And I have a feeling they may need our help."

11
The Search

SARA and Blair hurried down to the Prayer Rocks where Blair had parked the pickup. In a short time they were on their way up the highway.

"Why are we going this way?" Sara asked. "Isn't Homet's Ferry across the river?"

"It's on this side, too," Blair reminded her. "And we don't know what side of the river they're at. We'll check this side first because it's closer."

About a mile or two up the highway, Blair turned off on a narrow road that seemed to wind around endlessly through meadows and past farmhouses until at last they glimpsed the river through the trees. Blair parked alongside the road and led them past several summer cottages perched high on stilts.

"Why are these cottages built off the ground?" asked Sara curiously.

"Because of floods," Blair said. "The river gets pretty high here."

He turned in at a small white cottage. "I know the Keenans who live here," he said. "I'll ask if they saw Sam and Jim."

While he ran up the long flight of steps and knocked on the screen door, Sara looked around for a gray van. But she didn't see a van of any kind among the parked cars.

A pleasant-looking woman in jeans and a sweatshirt opened the door. She smiled at Blair and they talked for a few minutes. Then Blair waved good-bye and ran down the steps. He shrugged as he came up to where Sara was standing.

"No luck. Mrs. Keenan said she hasn't seen Sam or Jim. And nobody came to the landing this morning except a couple of fishermen she knows."

They walked down to the rocky landing and looked across the river. "Then Sam and Jim must be at Homet's Ferry on the other side," Sara reasoned.

"We'll paddle over," Blair said. "It's lots quicker that way."

Sara turned to Blair with surprise. "Paddle over?"

"Sure," Blair said grinning at her. "It just so happens that I keep my canoe here at this landing. You'll be getting that canoe ride I promised quicker than you thought."

He led the way across the landing to a row of overturned aluminum canoes.

"I know which one is yours," Sara said before Blair could point it out to her. "It's the canoe with the bright blue fleur-de-lis painted on each end of it."

Blair flashed her a smile. "Right. We all put insignias on

110

our canoes to show which one is ours. I thought the blue fleur-de-lis design would look kind of neat."

Sara smiled in agreement and helped Blair to turn the canoe upright. Underneath it were two paddles and four bright orange life vests.

"Do you know how to paddle?" Blair asked as he helped Sara fasten on one of the life vests.

"Well...." Sara answered uncertainly. Then she added quickly, "I know how to row a boat."

They carried the canoe across the landing and pushed it into the water. "Paddling's not that hard after you get the hang of it," Blair assured her. "Get in the front and I'll sit in back and steer."

He held the end while Sara stepped gingerly to the front of the swaying craft. When she was seated, Blair slipped into the rear seat and shoved off with his paddle.

Sara did a lot of splashing at first, but soon she mastered the long smooth strokes.

"Just dip the paddle into the water ahead of you and pull back with long, easy strokes," Blair instructed. "I'll do the guiding. Whatever you do, sit still and don't make any sudden movements. Canoes tip over easily."

"I can see that," Sara said in a shaky voice. She followed Blair's example and dipped her paddle into the water. She did a lot of splashing at first, but soon she mastered the long smooth strokes.

"We can't paddle directly across the river because of the riffles at the shoal," Blair called out. "So we'll paddle downstream then cross over at the bend where the current isn't so strong."

Sara, who was used to rowing a flat-bottomed boat on a small marsh pond at home, viewed the wide river ahead of her with awe. But Blair's skillful paddling gave her confidence, and soon she was enjoying riding the swift current downstream.

When they reached the bend, they crossed over to the opposite shore. The current was against them now as they made their way upriver to the landing. Encouraged by Blair's deep, strong strokes that pushed them forward, Sara dug her paddle deep into the current to help them along.

Ahead was the shoal and the eddy. Blair skillfully guided the canoe close to the shore so that they would avoid the riffles. At last they were in the calm waters of the inlet. Blair back-watered to bring his end of the canoe to the landing so that he could get out first and help Sara out. They pulled the canoe on shore, then looked around the rocky landing.

"Someone else is here," Sara remarked, pointing to an aluminum rowboat with an outboard motor in the stern. The motor was tilted out of the water and covered with a tarpaulin.

"There's no car around," Blair observed. "Probably some

112

fisherman from Frenchtown left his boat here so that he won't have to haul it when he comes again."

"Probably," Sara echoed.

They helped each other out of their life vests and started up the shadowy road from the landing. A heavy silence hung over the wooded promontory. Homet's Ferry was as deserted and lonely this afternoon as it had been when they were here before, thought Sara.

"If Sam and Jim are here," she half-whispered in the dim stillness, "I wonder where they are."

Blair shrugged. "Let's walk up the road. Maybe they didn't come down as far as the landing."

They walked past the stone wall with the commemorative millstone and followed the road that led to Frenchtown, a mile away. It was a warm, humid afternoon and the still air seemed to smother them. Mosquitoes and deer flies swarmed from the tall grass on either side of the road and hummed around their ears and stung their arms and bare ankles.

They walked past the abandoned farmhouse and on to where the gravel road turned to macadam and the houses of Frenchtown came into view. At the fork in the road, Blair stopped to wipe the beads of perspiration from his forehead. His flushed face tightened into a frown as he looked down at the white church and beyond it to the horseshoe curve of Azilum.

"There's no use going any farther. We're well out of bounds of Homet's Ferry. You know, I wonder if we read Sam's message correctly. I wonder if HF does mean Homet's Ferry."

Sara gave her head a grim nod. "I'm beginning to wonder the same thing." She groaned as she slapped at a whining insect about to light on her arm. "There doesn't seem to be

113

anything here but mosquitoes."

Blair let out a long sigh. "May as well head back to the landing."

As they started back, Sara had a thought. She wasn't about to give up on Sam and Jim yet.

"We have been walking in the middle of the road," she told Blair. "Let's walk back along the sides. We may just find something in the tall grass which will give us a clue to where they are."

Blair looked at the tall grass and weeds along the edges of the road which were powdered white from gravel dust. He doubted it, but he crossed the road to the opposite side to please Sara.

They retraced their steps, walking silently and keeping their eyes open for anything alongside of the road that might be a clue to what had happened to Sam and Jim.

As they walked along, Sara studied the dusty weeds and long grass so intently that after a while they became a blur. They were passing the old farmhouse and she was beginning to lose hope of finding a clue when she spied a flash of bright red color in a clump of ferns. Running into the dooryard, she stooped to part the ferns.

"Blair!" she shrilled. "I found something."

Blair came running. His eyes widened as he stared at the Indian moccasin. "It looks like Jim's," he exclaimed.

"I know it's Jim's," Sara said quickly as she reached into the ferns to pick up the moccasin. "I remember admiring the red-and-white-beaded bird design on his moccasins the first time we met him."

Blair glanced up at the old farmhouse. "Then this must be where they are," he said with a burst of confidence. "Come on, let's find out."

As they made their way across the weedy dooryard, they

found telltale signs that someone had been here recently. There were furrows through the long grass that led up to the house, and here and there a stray fern frond was bent.

They stepped up on the rickety wooden porch and peered through a crooked window frame. Inside the old house shreds of faded wallpaper hung from the walls of the front room. Along the side of one wall was the empty mouth of a charred fireplace. In the middle of the sagging floor leaned an abandoned chair with one leg broken and a rusty spring hanging out of its cushion. Most of the stuffing had been pulled out to make a rat's nest.

"Ugh," muttered Sara as she moved away from the window.

They walked over to the front door, its white paint gray and peeling. When Blair pushed on it, it creaked open on rusty hinges. Cautiously he stepped inside a dark hallway. He froze in his tracks.

"Yikes!" he cried out in alarm, warning Sara not to step through the missing floorboards.

They made their way around the gaping hole in the rotted floor to the back of the house where a rusty old sink hung along the outer wall and a black cast-iron stove squatted across from it. A heavy, musty silence hung over everything.

"Where can they be?" Blair wondered, looking around the empty kitchen.

"I don't know," Sara replied, pressing Jim's moccasin closer to her. "Let's call out for them."

At the top of their voices, they yelled, "Sam! Jim!"

They were answered only by the echoes of their voices that wafted through the empty rooms.

Blair walked across the slanted kitchen floor. At the far end was a door which opened on a winding stairway that fanned out along the outer wall. He motioned for Sara to

115

follow him as he started up the narrow, back stairs.

The old steps groaned and squeaked beneath their feet. At the top they stared into the shadows of a long hallway. Blair was about to start down the hall when Sara's hand gripped his arm. She pointed to something lying on the floor in front of them.

Blair picked it up and they bent their heads close together to examine it. It was a curl of rope that looked like a piece of clothesline.

"It's new," Blair said. "Look how white it is."

He was stuffing the rope into his pocket when Sara hissed, "Listen!"

They stood rigid, straining their ears. From somewhere along this dusky hall came a muffled sound. Sara couldn't figure it out. It didn't sound like an animal, yet it didn't sound quite human, either. It sounded like a ghostly moan, she thought.

She pointed to the room nearest them and quavered through tight lips, "It-it came from behind that door."

They crept along the hall and Blair opened the door slowly. A shiver traveled up the back of Sara's neck as she followed him into the room.

It was dark and had a stuffy, old-house smell as if it hadn't been aired for a long time. Blair moved toward the window and was about to throw up the blind so that they could see better when the muffled sound came again.

It was much louder this time, and they knew that it came from right here in this room.

Sara's courage seemed to ebb right out through her feet when Blair whispered in husky tones, "I just saw something move over there!"

12

Escape Down the River

SARA and Blair's first impulse was to run out of the room and into the hallway. But they stood their ground. There was something desperate about the muffled moan, as if someone was in distress.

"Somebody's in here," Sara said haltingly. "I'm sure of it now, and it sounds as if whoever it is needs help."

They forced themselves to walk slowly across the room toward the dark shape on the floor. Sara let out a gasp when the shape moved awkwardly toward her. It was not until Blair whipped up the window blind that she saw who it was.

"Sam!"

Her twin blinked his eyes in the sudden light and bobbed his head. Sitting up stiffly on the floor, he continued to inch

117

his way toward her by flexing up his legs and dragging himself forward on the seat of his pants. His ankles were tied with clothesline, as were his wrists behind his back. He could make only muffled sounds through the tape across his mouth. Jim was leaning against the wall on the far side of the room. He was trussed up the same way.

"Oh, Sam!" Sara moaned as she ripped the tape from his mouth and Blair worked at the knots in the rope.

When the two boys were untied, Sara and Blair helped them to their feet. Rubbing the circulation back into their wrists where the ropes had dug in, Sam and Jim gasped at the same time, "Thanks!"

Blair looked at the pair with astonishment. "How did you two ever get into such a hassle?"

"It's a long story," Sam said, "but here goes."

The boys took turns telling how they had found Princess Morning Star's missing pendant on the table inside Orme's trailer. They told how they had hidden the pendant when Mr. Cheney and Orme found them in the trailer and how, when they wouldn't tell the men where the fleur-de-lis pendant was hidden, they were bound and gagged and brought here.

Jim flexed his stiff arms and legs. "Old Cheney said he had heard about this abandoned house from some locals at the Marie Antoinette Lookout," he explained, "so he thought this would be a good place to hide us."

"And we thought we'd never get out of here until we heard you downstairs, calling our names," Sam put in. "We thought we'd go hoarse trying to make you hear us, but I guess you couldn't with us upstairs here, shut up in this room. It wasn't until we heard your footsteps on the squeaky old stairs that we knew we had a chance, so we moaned as loud as we could behind that awful tape."

118

"Where are Mr. Cheney and Orme now?" Sara asked, glancing anxiously toward the grimy window.

"They said something about going back to Orme's trailer and hunting for the pendant," Jim mumbled.

"They said if they don't find it soon, they'll be back to make us talk," Sam added.

"They won't find it in a hurry," Jim broke in. He looked at Sam and the two boys exchanged grins.

"What's so funny?" Sara demanded.

Amid the snickers, Jim said, "Sam stuck it at the bottom of a can of coffee."

"A can of coffee!" exclaimed Sara. "What a dopey place to hide it."

"It was the best place I could think of in a hurry," Sam said, dismissing the subject with a shrug. He added, "I guess you saw the letters I carved on the ground by the trailer step or you wouldn't be here."

Blair nodded. "We saw your initial on the ground, too. That was a neat clue, Sam."

"And we found your moccasin, Jim," Sara added, looking down at the moccasin she was still holding. "You slipped it off in the dooryard on purpose, didn't you?"

Jim nodded. "I kicked it off in that clump of ferns, hoping someone would see it."

Sara held out the moccasin and he took it gratefully, slipping it on his bare foot. "Orme must have thought it had come off in the van. Anyway, he didn't say anything when he tied my ankles."

Meanwhile Sam had moved over to the window and was keeping watch with anxious eyes through the dusty pane. "I think we should get out of here," he warned. "If they don't find the pendant. . . ."

He didn't finish the sentence, for at that moment they

119

heard the sound of a car coming down the road. The other three flew to the window and stared out.

"I hope it's just a fisherman!" Sara said in a frightened whisper.

Sam's hand reached for the green blind and drew it down over the pane but not before they glimpsed the familiar gray van speeding down the road in a cloud of dust.

"They sure returned in a hurry," Jim muttered.

Blair intervened, "Like Sam said, we better split. We can sneak out the back way and down to the landing."

"Why to the landing?" Sam whispered to Sara as they were fleeing down the back stairs.

"Blair has his canoe there," Sara returned in a hushed voice.

Blair paused for a second at the bottom of the steps. Then he waved them on. As they crept across the kitchen, they could hear the two men approaching the house.

"We'll make them talk," came Mr. Cheney's angry voice. "Before we finish with them, they'll tell us where they hid that pendant."

Sam drew in a quick breath. "Let's get out of here."

Blair yanked on the warped old kitchen door, forcing it open. It let out a loud squeak just as Mr. Cheney and Orme were entering the front of the house.

Not waiting to see if the men had heard the sound, Blair pulled Sara after him and the boys followed. They fled across the backyard and down a weedy slope that led to the inlet. As they neared the stony shore, they heard a thrashing in the tall grass behind them. A quick glance over their shoulders told them that Orme was following.

Blair reached the landing first and pushed the canoe into the water, waving the others into it. Quickly they piled in, pellmell over each other's heels. Sam clumsily tripped over

120

one of the thwarts, almost tipping them over. Sara made him sit down in the middle with her and be quiet. While they were fastening on their life vests, Blair pushed off with his paddle, just as Orme arrived at the landing.

As they drifted out of the inlet, the twins looked back over their shoulders to see what Orme was doing. The big man was standing in the middle of the landing, angry and bewildered as he watched the canoe float downstream with the current.

In desperation he looked around him and spying the motorboat, he hurried over to it. He pushed the boat into the river and got in. Pulling off the tarpaulin, he lowered the motor into running position and shoved the retaining pin in place. He set the throttle and pulled the starter lanyard several times until the motor caught with a puff of blue exhaust. With a roar the boat chugged out of the inlet after them.

All this time Blair and Jim were paddling hard, sending the canoe downriver on the swift current. In no time they reached the bend.

When Blair didn't turn to cross the river, Sara called back to him, "Aren't you going to cross over to Homet's Ferry on the other side?"

Blair shook his head and continued paddling downstream in swift strokes.

"But that's where we left the pickup," Sara protested.

Without breaking the rhythm of his paddling, Blair explained, "We couldn't make it across the current with Orme following. With the motor, he'd catch up with us and cut us off."

"Then where are we going?" asked Sam.

"Downriver," Blair replied. "I know a shortcut to the Prayer Rocks."

Sara was beginning to see the logic of Blair's thinking. Riding the swift current downstream, they seemed to be going as fast as the motorboat behind them. However, it wasn't long before the drone of the motor sounded nearer. Sara glanced fearfully over her shoulder. Orme was catching up.

"He's gaining on us," she shrilled. "What do we do now?"

"There's only one thing to do," Blair said grimly. "We'll have to try to make it across the river. There's a rift on the other side that motorboats steer clear of. If we can make it across to that rift, we'll be safe."

Using the paddle as a rudder, Blair turned the canoe skillfully and they swung out onto the broad crest of the river. Not far downstream, along the opposite shore, they could see the white water of the rift. If they could only make it in time!

But it wasn't long before they heard the loud drumming of the motor behind them. Orme had the motor going at full throttle. The aluminum boat was spanking the water as it gained on them.

Suddenly the canoe began to rock as the motorboat caught up with it and roared alongside. In a wide sweep to cut them off, Orme swung across their bow. The canoe tipped dangerously back and forth in the wake of the motor. Sara and Sam held their breath as they clung to the sides, saying silent prayers that they wouldn't capsize. Just in time, Blair dug his paddle into the current, steadied the canoe, and turned it toward shore again.

Now the waves from the wake slapped against the bow, slowing their progress and heaving their canoe up and down like a bouncing bronco. But just ahead lay the rift.

Orme must have seen the rift, too. He was just about to

make another sweep around them when he looked up with surprise and yelled out angrily. With a quick turn of the tiller, he swung the boat around and headed for the middle of the river and deeper water.

Blair and Jim bent their backs to the paddles and aimed straight for the rift. When the canoe reached the white water, Blair stopped paddling and used his paddle as a rudder again, guiding the canoe skillfully through the riffles. He's done this before, Sam thought, relieved that Blair knew the river so well.

When they reached the shallow water along the eastern bank, Jim looked up from his paddling to glance across the river. "He's not turned back," he warned. "He's following us from the middle of the river."

"We'll duck behind that island up ahead," Blair said. "He won't see us if we paddle down the inside channel. Just south of the island are the Prayer Rocks."

Soon the trees and bushes that hung over the channel hid them from view. When they drifted past the southern point of the island, Orme and the motorboat were no longer in sight.

Blair said with a relieved laugh, "He's probably around that bend downriver, hunting for us."

Only then did they relax their frantic paddling. "What I can't understand is why Orme and Mr. Cheney didn't split with Orme's trailer instead of messing around with us," Jim said curiously.

"Because they weren't sure we hid the pendant *inside* the trailer," Sam told him.

Jim blinked, puzzled. "I don't understand."

Sam went on to explain, "Well, we could have flung it out the trailer window when we saw them coming. For all they know, it may be lying somewhere in the woods."

"I hadn't thought of that," Jim said, frowning. "I guess that's why Orme is following us down the river. Now that we got away, he and Mr. Cheney are afraid we'll return to Spirit Lake and get the pendant."

Sam nodded grimly. "And I have the feeling that while Orme is trying to prevent us from getting to the trailer, Mr. Cheney is on his way to the council grounds in the van."

"Oh, wow, then we got to beat him to it," Jim said. "Where is that shortcut to the Prayer Rocks, Blair?"

In answer to Jim's question, Blair pointed with his paddle to the steep, wooded river bluff just ahead.

Jim stared incredulously at the cliff that sliced down in a sheer drop to the river. "You mean we have to climb *that*?"

"Don't worry. I know a way to get up it," Blair said. "A couple of years ago some guys and I made a switchback trail up to the Prayer Rocks from the river. If the trail is still there, we're in."

While they continued paddling downriver toward the cliff, the still, humid afternoon suddenly darkened. A cool wind now blew across the river. Sara glanced at the sky. Black rain clouds were piling up on the horizon. A low rumble of thunder sounded over the tops of the distant mountains.

"I think it's going to storm!" she called out in warning.

"It looks that way," Blair called back. "Come on, Jim, let's paddle harder. We're almost at the Rocks."

Minutes later, Blair pointed the bow in toward shore, and they could see the jagged edge of the overhanging rocks high up through the trees. Just as the canoe nudged the stony shore, they heard the sound of a motor coming up the river.

Blair looked up with alarm. "Orme's probably heading upriver because of the storm. Hurry up! Help me get this canoe pulled up on shore under those bushes."

As they helped him hide the canoe, the sound of the motor grew louder. Orme must have seen them, for now the motorboat was turning in toward shore.

"Follow me," Blair called out. He had already started up a thin trail that slanted upward along the steep bluff.

They ran for the cover of trees where they quickly removed their life vests and hid them under some bushes along the trail. Then they started up the awesome switchback after Blair.

The trail was overgrown in many places, and they had to push their way through tangles of vines and bushes. Halfway up, a rock slide blocked their way so that they had to scramble over slippery, moss-covered boulders to get back on the trail. It was good the trail was a switchback, Sam thought, otherwise they could never have made it to the top.

Through the thick foliage below them they couldn't see if Orme was following. They couldn't hear his footsteps, either, in the rising wind that thrashed the leaves around them and roared through the hemlocks. They could only hope that if Orme was following, he was far enough behind them so that they could reach the trailer first and have time to rescue the pendant.

"We're halfway up," Blair shouted, encouraging Sara and Sam who were several yards behind.

His words were echoed by a loud clap of thunder that seemed to shake the entire cliff. The gust of wind that followed slashed the treetops and tore at the bushes alongside the trail.

"Hurry up!" Sam called out as he pushed Sara over a fallen limb. They were on their hands and knees now, clutching at rocks and pulling themselves up by slanting tree trunks as they neared the top of the bluff.

As if the steep climb wasn't bad enough, the black, rain-swollen clouds finally let go and a torrent poured down on them as Blair and Jim finally reached the top and pulled the twins over the steep edge of the cliff and into the shelter of an overhanging rock.

They sank down on the floor of the shelter, gulping in great lungsful of air. They were soaked to the skin, the raindrops running down their hair and dripping off their clothes. Sara glanced ruefully at her muddy jeans and canvas shoes.

They had scarcely caught their breath when Blair announced, "Let's go. We can't waste anymore time."

They scrambled out from underneath the ledge and in the downpour clambered up the wet path that led to the turnout. As the storm hovered over them, it was almost as black as night, the bluff brightened only now and then by flashes of lightning that gave the rocks and trees and bushes around them a surrealistic look.

Sara wondered where Orme was in all this downpour. Was he climbing the switchback trail or had he decided to wait out the storm in the motorboat? At least the storm was hindering his progress as much as theirs.

When they reached the highway, Jim suggested the quickest way to Spirit Lake was the road he and Sam had taken in Mr. Cheney's van. They walked the quarter mile down the highway, then up the steep gravel road that led to the clearing. By the time they had staggered up to the trailer, the sky brightened and the rain was now a drizzle.

"We beat them to it," Jim crowed triumphantly, relieved to find that Mr. Cheney's van hadn't arrived yet.

"Yeah," Sam said, "but we'll have to get the pendant in a hurry. They could be here any minute."

"Just grab that coffee can and let's beat it," Blair intervened, looking warily back at the road they had just climbed.

Sam and Jim ran up to the trailer door. But instead of flinging it open, they began pulling frantically at it.

"It's locked!" cried Jim.

"Oh, wow!" Blair moaned.

They all took a turn at rattling the doorknob, but it was futile. Orme had locked his trailer this time.

"If we had a piece of wire or a coat hanger, maybe we could force the lock," Sara suggested desperately.

"I could run to my trailer and get a coat hanger," Jim offered.

Blair shook his head. "That would take too long."

"I got it!" Sam exclaimed with a snap of his fingers. "Your dad's gasoline credit card, Blair. It's stiff plastic, and I read somewhere that if you wedge it into the crack of a door, you can force the lock open. Do you have it with you?"

"Sure," Blair said, reaching into his hip pocket for his wallet. "I always carry it with me when I'm driving the pickup."

He brought out his wallet and was fumbling through the cards when they heard the groan of an engine and the scrunch of tires on the steep gravel road behind them.

"Oh, no!" groaned Jim.

"Quick!" warned Sam. "Hide back in the woods."

Blair jammed his wallet back into his pocket and they made a dash for a clump of hemlocks several yards away from the trailer. Sara's heart lurched when, through the green boughs, she glimpsed Mr. Cheney's van lumbering up the road toward them.

13
Searching for Help

MR. Cheney got out of the van and paused for a moment as he studied the trailer. He began walking around it, kicking up leaves and stooping now and then to peer into the bushes alongside it. He's still looking for the pendant, Sara thought. Sam was right. Mr. Cheney was not sure the boys had hidden it inside the trailer.

A raindrop fell on her neck and trickled coldly down her back. She wanted to hunch her shoulders and squirm, but she didn't dare to move with Mr. Cheney nearby.

Just as he was finishing his circle around the trailer, a very wet, bedraggled Orme came floundering into the clearing.

Mr. Cheney looked up with surprise. "Where did you come from, Orme?" he called out.

Orme shuffled wearily up to the van. Waving his hands and exclaiming, he muttered a jumble of words they couldn't understand. They knew, though, by his gestures that he was relating his experiences of pursuing them down the river. Mr. Cheney didn't seem too happy with the news. He kept looking around with furtive glances.

Under the dripping hemlocks, Sam leaned close to Sara and said in an urgent whisper, "He thinks we're around here somewhere. See if you can get to the council grounds without being seen. Find Jim's father. And hurry. We guys will try to detain them until you get help."

Sara nodded. She wanted to warn Sam, but she knew it was too risky to say anything more, and every minute counted. Silently she slipped back through the wet woods.

She circled the pond bank until she came to the path that led to the council grounds. No one was in sight as she hurried up to Jim's trailer. Anxiously she knocked on the small white door. She waited for what seemed an eternity, knocking again several more times.

When she was sure nobody was there, she swung around to survey the craft cabins. If she couldn't find Chief Sun Bear, she would have to find someone else to help her.

But the council grounds were empty, the tourists seeking shelter from the shower in their cars and the council members closing their stands and waiting out the storm in their trailers.

Desperately she hurried along the line of trailers. If she did not get help quickly, Mr. Cheney and Orme might get away in the trailer with Princess Morning Star's pendant and the boys might be in trouble trying to stop them.

"Oh, please, God, let someone be here," she prayed as she flung herself at Princess Morning Star's trailer door and rapped frantically.

As if in answer to her prayer, the door swung open and the Indian woman stood there, staring with surprise at the wet, disheveled girl in front of her. "Why, it's Sara! My goodness, come in out of the rain."

As Sara stepped inside the trailer, David Greenleaf joined his wife. They listened intently while Sara, in a rush of words, poured out her story.

When she finished, David said, "I never did trust Orme."

"I know," Princess Morning Star replied sadly. "You mentioned just last night that he needs guidance and suggested that we try to bring God into his life."

While they were talking, David slipped into a raincoat, and Princess Morning Star hung a warm shawl around Sara's shoulders. The Indian woman begged Sara to remain in the trailer while David went to Spirit Lake, but Sara shook her head.

"I have to find out if Sam and the others are all right," she gasped. And before Princess Morning Star could protest further, Sara slipped out of the trailer with David.

As they passed the longhouse, two young men stepped out and waved to David. When David motioned for them to follow, they came along, and as Sara led the way through the wet woods, David filled them in on where they were going.

By the time they reached Spirit Lake, the storm had moved on and a watery sun had popped out from underneath a cloud. It shone on the dark waters of the pond and on the white travel trailer Sara pointed out to the men. She was relieved that the trailer was still in the clearing. But what was that loud pounding sound coming from inside it?

The men had heard the sound, too. They looked at one another with alarm, then hurried around the pond bank and into the clearing. When they arrived at the trailer, they

The three boys relaxed their hold on the door. The next moment a very angry Orme burst from the trailer.

gaped in astonishment at the three boys leaning hard against the door to keep it shut.

Sara cried out, "Sam, what are you doing?"

Her twin looked around and when he caught a glimpse of David and the men, he grinned with relief. "Are we glad to see you!" He had to shout over the loud pounding on the other side of the door. "We've got Orme in here and he's determined to get out."

"No telling how long we could have kept him inside," Jim gasped.

"Well, you can leave everything up to us now," David told the boys.

With those welcome words all three relaxed their hold on

131

the door, and the next moment a very angry Orme burst out of the trailer, tumbled down the step, and landed on the ground in front of David and his two stalwart friends. The three men closed in on their prisoner with grim, determined faces.

Sara glanced quickly around the clearing. "Where's Mr. Cheney?" she piped. She had noticed for the first time that the gray van was gone.

"He got away," Blair informed her.

"Got away!" Sara screeched. "How did that happen?"

Blair frowned down at the big Indian. "Orme here was all for looking around the trailer some more for the pendant," he answered, "but Mr. Cheney was getting nervous about hanging around. He said they couldn't risk searching anymore for the pendant with us on the loose to squeal on them. He said he was clearing out and that Orme had better do the same."

Blair paused for breath and Jim took up the story. "Orme said that Mr. Cheney should go on ahead and he'd meet him up the road with the trailer. Then we heard Mr. Cheney start up the van and leave. Soon after that Orme gave up searching outside the trailer and went inside. It was then that Sam got the bright idea of holding the door shut to keep him in there until you guys came."

All this time Orme was listening to what was said with a furious scowl on his face.

Jim couldn't resist a triumphant grin. "Would you like to know where Sam hid Princess Morning Star's pendant that you and Mr. Cheney stole?"

The big man didn't answer but scowled deeper as he watched Jim enter the trailer. A minute later the scowl turned to a look of astonishment as Jim held out the large can of coffee.

132

Jim dug down into the grains of coffee, and when he brought out the fleur-de-lis pendant, one of David's friends burst out laughing. "You would have had to drink a lot of coffee to find what was hidden in there, Orme."

The other young man gave Orme a fierce look and said, "Let's get him to the longhouse. The Grand Council will know what to do with him." He grabbed Orme by the arm and helped him to his feet.

The big man held back. "What about Hugh Cheney?" he protested. "He was in on this, too. In fact it was all his idea."

"The state police will pick him up where he planned to meet you," David said grimly. "He won't get far."

"You bet he won't," Sam said under his breath to Sara as they started back to the council grounds with their prisoner. "I memorized his license number."

14
The Lost Heirloom

"I sure hope Princess Morning Star's fleur-de-lis pendant is the lost heirloom," Blair said the next morning as they sat on the veranda and waited anxiously for their guests to arrive.

Mr. LaRue had invited Princess Morning Star, David Greenleaaf, Chief Sun Bear, and Jim Little Hawk for lunch so that they could compare the fleur-de-lis pendants. Princess Morning Star said she would be wearing hers, and Mr. LaRue got his out of the locked desk drawer so that it would be ready when their guests arrived.

Sara flashed Blair a look of confidence. "I'm sure it's the lost heirloom, Blair. When Princess Morning Star showed me her pendant that day in the craft cabin, it looked exactly like your dad's."

"Here they come!" Sam broke in as Chief Sun Bear's car appeared on the drive.

Blair and the twins ushered their friends into the study where Mr. LaRue greeted them. Professor and Mrs. Harmon came in from the garden to join the gathering.

After seating his guests, Mr. LaRue took up the flat, velvet-covered jewel box that held Claude's fleur-de-lis pendant. "Now we can compare the pendants," he told Princess Morning Star. "Would you care to take yours off and bring it over here to the light?"

The Indian princess unfastened the gold chain around her neck and placed the pendant on the desk next to Mr. LaRue's.

"I don't think I'll ever let this pendant out of my sight again," she said.

They gathered around in a tight little group and stared down at the two pendants. The three gold petals of the two fleur-de-lis were identical, even to the ends that were visible below the horizontal band that held them together. Mr. LaRue brought out a magnifying glass and turned both pendants over. "Now we will see for sure," he said. "According to Claude's journal, the jeweler's mark is inscribed faintly on the back of each one."

Sara's hazel eyes were shining with excitement as she watched their host squint through the glass at Princess Morning Star's fleur-de-lis and then at his own. When he straightened up, he exclaimed with a broad smile, "They are both alike."

"I knew it!" Sara cried, hopping up and down and smiling over at Blair.

Blair grinned back at her with relief.

Mr. LaRue turned to Princess Morning Star. His round face was flushed with happiness. "I have found Jacques' descendant at last! Welcome to his family, my dear."

He gave the Indian princess a warm embrace. Then Blair, beaming, hugged her, too. Sara felt tears of emotion well up in her eyes at the happy family reunion.

"I will see that you get Jacques' inheritance as soon as possible," Mr. LaRue said. "This afternoon, right after lunch, we'll pay a visit to my lawyer."

"Wow, is she going to be rich?" Jim blurted out.

"It is a tidy sum," Mr. LaRue told him.

"Whatever amount it is, I will use it to help our people on the reservations," Princess Morning Star replied.

Mr. LaRue smiled his approval. "I am sure Jacques would have liked that." He paused with a blissful sigh. "I am so glad that, after all these years, we have found Jacques' descendant and that I can fulfill Claude's wishes in his will. Do you know that this is the first time in two centuries that the LaRues are united into one happy family again? How pleased Claude would be."

"I am sure Jacques would be pleased, too," Princess Morning Star said, her eyes glistening with happiness.

At that moment Abby McGuire announced lunch. Mr. LaRue put his arms around both Princess Morning Star and David and led the way into the dining room. While they ate Mrs. McGuire's delicious ham loaf and pineapple salad, they discussed the happenings of yesterday.

"What happened after we left the council grounds?" Blair asked eagerly. "Did the state police find Mr. Cheney?"

Chief Sun Bear nodded gravely. "The state troopers found his van on a side road off Route 6, where he and Orme had planned to meet. He is now in custody. As for Orme, we asked the magistrate if our tribe could deal with him in our own way. The courts know that David and Princess Morning Star have done good work with criminal offenders on the reservations, and I believe they will be given custody of Orme."

"We would like to take Orme with us on our mission work and try to rehabilitate him," David told them. "We feel that he is not a hardened criminal, just a weak man who needs guidance. If Orme becomes involved in helping others, we believe that he will find God and learn to lead a useful life."

"Yesterday at the council meeting he broke down and told us everything that had happened," Princess Morning Star added, "and that is a good beginning."

Chief Sun Bear nodded his agreement. "Yes, he told us that four days ago Mr. Cheney had found him at our council and told him that he had another job for him. They knew each other because Mr. Cheney had used Orme's help several times in the past in his shady business dealings."

"Shady business dealings," Mr. LaRue echoed thoughtfully. "I can believe that. This morning I investigated our Mr. Cheney by calling a friend of mine in New York who deals in antique jewelry. I was informed that Hugh Cheney is an unscrupulous dealer. He had evidently heard from the other dealers that I was looking for Jacques' fleur-de-lis pendant. I believe that's why he was eavesdropping on us— to find out what the pendant looked like, so that if he found it, he could sell it to me for a large sum of money. Unfortunately, he happened to be snooping around the very day I was showing it to the Harmons and telling them about Jacques' inheritance."

"That's what he told Orme," Princess Morning Star said. "And then the next day when he saw that I was wearing an identical pendant, he must have realized that it was Jacques' long-lost fleur-de-lis pendant. When I wouldn't sell him the pendant, he talked Orme into stealing it."

"Orme is a council member and has access to the area

where we park our campers and travel trailers," David went on to explain. "He found our trailer and waited until we had left it. Then he searched the trailer, found the jewel case, and stole the pendant. It was all done quickly, that same afternoon."

"So that's what happened to the missing pendant!" Sara put in. "But what I can't understand is why Mr. Cheney and Orme didn't leave Wyalusing as soon as they had the pendant. Why hang around to get caught?"

"We wondered about that, too," Chief Sun Bear replied. "When we asked Orme the reason, he said that after Mr. Cheney had overheard Mr. LaRue tell about Jacques' inheritance, he got the idea of posing as Jacques LaRue's heir. He thought Jacques' inheritance would be worth considerably more than he could get from simply selling the pendant. But he didn't want to approach Mr. LaRue as Jacques' missing heir until Princess Morning Star and David left Wyalusing."

"Of course not," reasoned Sam. "Princess Morning Star and David could expose him."

"Which you boys did in the end when you found my pendant in Orme's trailer," Princess Morning Star pointed out. "Mr. Cheney then decided that he'd have to sell the pendant on the black market and get away from Wyalusing as soon as he and Orme found where you two hid the pendant."

She smiled at the boys. "But they never did find it."

Jim piped up, "We guys can't take all the credit for solving the mystery. Orme said that when Mr. Cheney found Sara spying around his cabin at the Marie Antoinette Lookout, he knew that she was on to something, too."

Mrs. Harmon looked up with surprise. "Sara spying around Mr. Cheney's cabin at the lookout?"

Sara blushed then quickly confessed to her mother what she had been up to the day they had lunch at the Lookout. "I know it wasn't right snooping around like that," she added, "but Mr. Cheney was acting so strangely when we saw him with Orme at the Prayer Rocks that I had to find out more about him."

"And you did," Sam spoke up loyally. "You found his business card that told us he was an antique jewelry dealer. That really made us suspicious."

"What I can't understand," Blair said with a puzzled shake of his head, "is why Mr. Cheney didn't hide the pendant in his cabin at the Lookout instead of in Orme's trailer."

"We asked Orme about that, too," David Greenleaf replied. "He said that Mr. Cheney thought the cabin at the Lookout would be too public, with the maid coming in every day to make the bed and everything. So that's why he asked Orme to hide it in his trailer at Spirit Lake."

Sam grinned knowingly. "And that's why Mr. Cheney kept a close watch on Orme's trailer the night of the tribal dances."

Jim nodded. "Orme told us that Mr. Cheney insisted on staying at the trailer while Orme went to the dances. When Mr. Cheney heard us in the clearing at Spirit Lake, he quickly turned off the light in the trailer so that we wouldn't see him. With the pendant there, he didn't like the idea of kids prowling around and decided to frighten us away from Spirit Lake once and for all. So, remembering what Orme had told him about the legend of Spirit Lake, he slipped out of the trailer and went to the longhouse. In the crowds and the excitement of the dances, no one noticed him sneak in and take the ugliest mask on the wall."

Sara's eyes widened. "So it was Mr. Cheney who used

139

that medicine mask to frighten us away from Spirit Lake!"

Jim nodded. "Mr. Cheney was our ghost. The legend of Spirit Lake is still just a legend, Sara."

They were all quiet for a moment, then Sam said with satisfaction, "Well, I guess that covers everything. I can't think of anything else to figure out."

"Neither can I," Sara said with a feeling of relief.

Professor Harmon, who had been listening with interest to what was being said, now spoke up with a smile. "Well, it looks as if you have your mystery solved, Charles."

Mr. LaRue leaned back in his chair, his eyes twinkling. "I must say, John, that I'm not surprised with your two sleuths as our guests."

All eyes turned gratefully to Sara and Sam. Sara felt her cheeks grow warm and Sam grinned self-consciously. Mr. LaRue's praise made them happy, but at the same time it made them feel a little uncomfortable.

"We couldn't have solved the mystery without Blair's expert handling of the canoe and his help in climbing the river bluff," Sam pointed out generously. "That was some escape downriver."

"Jim's knowledge of the council grounds and spying on Orme helped a lot, too," Sara added, with a look of admiration for the Indian boy.

Jim flashed her a smile, then looked eagerly at his father. "Can we tell them now, Dad?" he asked.

With a gleam of laughter in his eyes, Chief Sun Bear replied, "After that question, Jim, they'll be dying of curiosity if we don't. Suppose you tell them, son."

"Okay," Jim said. He cleared his throat, then announced solemnly, "Sara, Sam, and Blair, because you have solved the mystery of Princess Morning Star's missing fleur-de-lis pendant and have brought much happiness to our Grand

Council, the chiefs and head women would like to adopt you into the Susquehannock Tribe in a ceremony to take place tomorrow at the longhouse. You will be brothers and a sister to our people for as long as you live."

For a moment the twins and Blair were too dumbfounded to speak. Then Blair exclaimed, "Oh, wow, that's neat!"

Princess Morning Star smiled at him with warm affection. "You have taken me into your family, Blair, and now I shall take you into mine."

Sara and Sam looked at one another and beamed. Little had they dreamed that by solving one of their mysteries they would have the honor of being adopted into a North American Indian tribe.

"It's the nicest thing that could ever happen to us," Sara murmured happily as she looked at the smiling faces around her.

Ruth Nulton Moore, born in Easton, Pennsylvania, taught English and social studies in schools in Pennsylvania and Michigan. Along with producing poetry and stories for children's magazines, she has written thirteen juvenile novels. Several of her books have been translated into other languages and are sold in England, Sweden, Finland, Germany, and Puerto Rico, as well as in the United States and Canada.

Mrs. Moore lives in Bethlehem, Pennsylvania, with her husband, who is a professor of accounting at Lehigh University. They have two grown sons and a granddaughter.

When she is not at her typewriter, Mrs. Moore is busy lecturing about the art of writing to students in public and Christian schools and colleges in her area.

Mrs. Moore is a member of Children's Authors and Illustrators of Philadelphia. Her biography appears in *The International Authors and Writers Who's Who*, 1982, and *Pennsylvania Women in History*, 1983.

Moore's children's novel, *Danger in the Pines*, received the C. S. Lewis Honor Book Medal as one of the top five children's books with a Christian message published in 1983. Another novel, *In Search of Liberty*, won the 1984 Silver Angel Award from Religion in Media.

The Moores own 46 acres of land in the Endless Mountains where they vacation on summer weekends.